PETAL TO THE METAL

THE BLOOMIN' PSYCHIC, BOOK 1

ANNABEL CHASE

Copyright © 2020 by Red Palm Press LLC

All rights reserved.

No part of this book may be reproduced in any form or by any electronic or mechanical means, including information storage and retrieval systems, without written permission from the author, except for the use of brief quotations in a book review.

Cover design by Ebook Launch

❦ Created with Vellum

CHAPTER ONE

Pellets of rain smacked me in the face as I made my way to the office on 53rd and Broadway. Spring in New York City wasn't all outdoor seating and strolls through Central Park, not when the damp air chilled me to the bone. I wish I'd worn my false lashes today. They'd behave like sexy soldiers, protecting my eyeballs from the invading droplets.

I was relieved when my client cancelled our appointment first thing this morning. I'd tossed and turned last night, unable to sleep for some unidentifiable reason. A late-night search on the internet narrowed the options down to perimenopause or pregnancy. It felt strange to be at an age where it could be either one. The morning brought clarity and I'd realized it was likely anxiety, knowing what was on my agenda later today.

I'd been tempted to stay in the apartment and watch Bravo reruns for an hour after the client's cancellation, but I thought it best to get to the office sooner rather than later. I did, however, linger in Starbucks for an extra twenty minutes while I sipped a latte and read Page Six on my phone. I fidgeted in my chair as I reviewed the latest scandals, eagerly anticipating the rest of the day. I'd decided to take advantage of the absence of my no-nonsense boss. Associate Publisher Lynette Regal was in Austin this week for an annual film festival. She ruled over our department with an iron fist, the kind of woman who made grown men weep into the sleeves of their Gucci dress shirts and babies long to crawl back into the womb. I swore up and down to my boyfriend Andrew that I once saw a Christmas cactus wilt in her presence, but he didn't believe me.

At the thought of Andrew, a smile formed on my lips. Today would be one for the memory books. I'd arranged for him to meet me in the lobby at two o'clock under the guise of going for coffee. Little did he know…

The cubicles were mostly empty when I arrived on the eleventh floor. It seemed the other salespeople were either meeting with clients or sheltering from the rain in their apartments. I couldn't see past the partition to the editorial department, although I could hear the voice of the New York bureau chief. Steve Bamberger always spoke about five decibels louder than everybody else. I suspected he had an undiagnosed hearing issue. Steve was in his late fifties and I got the impression that no one told him what to do, whether it was in his best interest or not.

I rounded the corner and was disappointed to see Carole Salisbury at her desk. The older woman was my immediate neighbor in the office, so naturally she'd be the one who decided to make an appearance this morning. I was hoping to have a little downtime and plan for the afternoon's event, but Carole harbored an unhealthy fear of our boss and was therefore eager to throw anyone under the bus if it kept Carole out of the doghouse for the day. It didn't matter that Lynette was away. The brickhouse of a woman could pester and bully her staff from any distance thanks to modern technology.

"Hey," I said, brushing past Carole's desk to reach mine. I dumped my bag on the floor and dropped into the chair. I wasn't a fan of morning chitchat and it was hard to stop Carole's mouth from moving once it started.

"That's some serious rain, huh?" Carole asked. She immediately spun around in her chair to engage me in conversation. Great.

"I narrowly avoided a puddle on the corner," I said. The well-dressed guy standing next to me got splashed by a passing cab—RIP Dolce & Gabbana loafers.

"I'm excited for this afternoon," Carole said. "I've been practicing in my apartment before bed. The cats don't like it, though. They hide when they hear the music."

"Andrew thinks I've joined a dance class," I said. "He has no idea what I've been planning." He left for work before I was awake this morning, so I was able to squeeze in another practice run on my own.

"I think it's a fun idea. I'm so glad you got so many of us involved." She snorted awkwardly. "I don't think I'll want to watch myself on the video though."

"You're on the far end," I reminded her. "If you want to avoid seeing yourself, it should be easy enough."

"I still can't believe you roped Steve and Monica into it," Carole said.

I smiled. "I can be charming when I want to be." It was how I'd managed to survive in sales for as long as I had. The only reason Carole was still here was because she knew where all the bodies were buried. Lynette relied on her more than she would ever admit, but Carole was one of those women who didn't recognize her worth and Lynette was more than happy to exploit that weakness. Poor Carole had a habit of diving beneath her desk and huddling into a ball whenever Lynette arrived in the office. For an arthritic woman in her sixties, her lightning-quick movements never failed to impress me. As far as I knew, she'd never once pulled a muscle.

I went through the motions of the day, calling clients and scheduling appointments, but my mind was on the afternoon. I hoped the rain didn't keep people out of the office or it would ruin the plan. I wasn't the most organized person in the world, except when it came to planning something fun. If you needed to organize a bachelorette party, I was your woman. At forty-two, I'd planned enough of them to consider myself a professional. Always a bridesmaid and never a bride, not that I'd been bothered by it. I'd always known my time would come eventually. My mother was on her third marriage and it seemed to me that practice did not, in fact, make perfect.

I scarfed down a bowl of minestrone soup for lunch and tried not to splatter it on my clothes. I didn't want my penchant for sloppiness to be memorialized onscreen. As more people trickled into the office, I started to relax. Everything was going to work out, no matter what the persistent voice in my head told me.

At two o'clock, I made my way down to the lobby where everyone had arranged to meet. Tricia, one of the administrative assistants, had agreed to handle the recording because she'd broken her leg skiing in January and wasn't able to participate. I knew we'd want a memento of the occasion.

By the time we were all assembled in the lobby, I counted twenty-five people. I waved to Rhonda from accounting, who was decked out in a hot pink tracksuit, ready for her closeup. Half of the participants I only knew by name because we rarely socialized. Salespeople weren't allowed to fraternize with the editorial staff, so a single dance routine would be the closest thing to a bonding experience we'd ever have. The security guards were kind enough to section off an area for us so that no one walked through at an inopportune moment. No one except Andrew, of course.

The seconds ticked by and there was no sign of him. I checked my phone for messages. Seeing none, I called and threw in another text for good measure. The rain would make it more difficult for him to arrive in midtown at this time of day. I just had to be patient.

Monica checked her watch. "I'm going to need to go in a few minutes. I have an interview scheduled."

As I was about to throw in the towel, I spotted Andrew's head bobbing between two others on its way toward the revolving door.

"Hit it!" I called over my shoulder.

I hurriedly took my place front and center and signaled for everyone to begin. The song I'd chosen was *I'm So Excited* by The Pointer Sisters. Andrew and I didn't have a song per se, but I figured if I was going to propose, then choosing a song that expressed excitement about marrying him was the right call.

The revolving door spit Andrew into the lobby, where he stopped dead in his tracks at the sight of us. Everyone within earshot gathered around to watch the flash mob in action. It was exhilarating and I enjoyed every second of it, even when I tweaked my lower back on one of the turns. The ibuprofen and heating pad later would be worth it.

The final moment had me sliding on my knees to land in front of Andrew while the four dancers behind me each held up a sign with a single word that amounted to Will You Marry Me?

I ignored the sharp pain in my left knee and beamed up at a slack-jawed Andrew.

"What is all this?" he asked.

Not the reaction I'd hoped for.

"What does it look like? It's a flash mob proposal." I

remained on my knees, mainly because I couldn't get up without help.

Andrew took a step backward, two bright spots forming on his cheeks. "I thought we were meeting for coffee. I had something to discuss with you."

"I guess that something wasn't marriage." My stomach began to churn. It seemed that my incredible idea wasn't so incredible after all. I heard someone tell Tricia to stop filming.

"I need to go," Andrew said. "This was a mistake." He turned and nearly got stuck in the revolving door in his haste to escape.

I felt a hand slide under my armpit and help me to my feet.

"Thank you, everyone," I said weakly. I followed the herd back to the elevator bank and stuffed myself between two of the reporters. I held my breath to avoid the stench of body odor.

I returned to my desk in a haze of disappointment and humiliation.

"You caught him by surprise, that's all," Carole said. "He probably wanted to be the one to propose."

"Yes, I'm sure that's it." But I wasn't sure at all. The look in Andrew's eyes…

"I think we should do a flash mob with Santa hats and make it our holiday video next year."

"It's March. Plenty of time to plan that one." The back of my neck began to bother me. It felt like a dozen tiny needles pricking my skin. Maybe I'd tweaked more than my lower back without realizing it.

"Are you okay?" Carole asked. "You look pale."

I rubbed the back of my neck in an effort to ease the discomfort. "I'll be fine."

She handed me a bottled water from her desk drawer. "Here. Drink this."

As I unscrewed the lid, I heard Steve's voice from the other side of the partition.

"It was only harmless fun, Lynette," he said, and my stomach plummeted.

Carole swiveled around to look at me, the color draining from her face. How could Lynette have gotten wind of it already?

Carole and I stared at the phone on my desk, waiting for it to ring.

"It wasn't anything official," I heard Steve say. Protecting his sources was second nature to him and I was grateful for the instinct. "I don't see what the big deal is. I'm the bureau chief and I have no problem with it, so I don't get why you should care."

I closed my eyes and swore under my breath. I thought we'd dodge the Lynette bullet but apparently not. The woman had eyes and ears everywhere.

Steve slammed down the phone and called Lynette a few choice names.

"Thanks, Steve," I yelled.

"You're not out of the woods yet," he called back. "You know Lynette. She's like a dog with a bone."

He wasn't wrong. Her nickname in certain circles was 'the pit bull,' which I considered an insult to pit bulls.

Carole's phone rang—not the landline but her cell phone. Her hands began to shake.

"Don't answer it," I said.

Carole's hand hovered over the phone. "I can't ignore her."

"You can," I said. "Pretend you're in the bathroom. No one answers the phone in the bathroom."

"I do when it's Lynette," Carole admitted.

Of course she did.

The ringing stopped and we breathed a collective sigh of relief—until my phone lit up.

I'd just had a marriage proposal rejected by my boyfriend. Did I really need to deal with one of Lynette's tantrums too?

"Here we go." I clicked the screen. "Hey, Lynette. How are you?"

"How do you think I am after what I just saw?"

"I feel like I should be the one saying that."

"Karaoke at the holiday party wasn't enough for you, was it? This company doesn't exist to be your personal playground, you know." She didn't give me a chance to respond. Her tirade included more swear words than a Jersey shore party. There were also accusations of destroying the integrity of the paper and making a mockery of her.

"I don't see why you're so angry about this," I managed to interrupt.

"We're the most respected entertainment publication in the business and you've reduced us to a laughingstock on social media," she screamed.

I rubbed my forehead, confused. "Social media? I didn't post this anywhere. It was meant to be private." Private humiliation, as it turned out.

"Carole shared it on Twitter and tagged me," Lynette said.

I glared at Carole. "Carole uploaded it *and* tagged you?" I repeated slowly.

Carole froze, her face flushed with guilt. "Oops."

"Life is not a cabaret, Amelia. Actions have consequences. I've been willing to overlook your shortcomings because you get results, but the time has come."

I shot Carole an exasperated look as Steve rounded the corner to watch the showdown.

"It's bad enough that you showed editorial and advertising in cahoots like that. There are long-established rules at this company," she continued.

"We weren't in cahoots. We also had accounting and administrative assistants involved," I said.

"No one will care. It calls our integrity into question and I can't abide that. You're fired."

My throat went dry. "Fired?" I croaked.

"I'm calling security to escort you out. You've embarrassed this company beyond belief. You'll never work in this town again after this debacle, Amelia Thorne."

"But it was only a flash mob…"

Lynette hung up.

Slowly, I lowered the phone to the desk, staring vacantly ahead.

"Mia, I'm so sorry," Carole said. "I uploaded the fun part, not what happened afterward. I never get to do stuff like this and I wanted to show people…"

"It's not your fault."

"I wasn't thinking. I always tag her on Twitter. It was an autopilot click."

I couldn't blame Carole. I was the organizer. The instigator. The troublemaker. The rabble rouser. I figured if Lynette found out at some point that she'd call me into her office and give me a firm dressing down, maybe take away a lucrative client to prove a point before congratulating me on my impending nuptials. I expected her to throw me an engagement party, not to fire me.

Steve dragged a hand through his thinning hair. "I'm so sorry, Mia. Lynette is being ridiculous, as always. Let me call Bob and talk to him on your behalf."

Even the Publisher himself couldn't save me now. Once you were in Lynette's bad graces, the best thing to do was exit stage left before she made your life a living hell. I'd seen it enough times to know.

"It's fine. I shouldn't have used company resources for a personal matter."

Kimberly from Human Resources approached us with an empty cardboard box. "I understand you need this, Amelia?" She set the box on my desk. "Let me know if you need any help. Security will escort you out when you're finished."

Kimberly had axed enough employees on Lynette's behalf to show no emotion. She hadn't been a part of the flash mob either, so she didn't share the guilt that Steve and Carole probably felt.

The Walk of Shame seemed to take an eternity. I walked past the rows of cubicles to the elevator bank, which seemed to stop on every floor before it reached me, prolonging my agony. No one spoke to me. They were all too afraid of guilt by association. Lynette once fired someone in the elevator because she disliked the smell of his aftershave. I don't know why I thought I was immune. Well, my hubris finally caught up with me.

I emerged from the lobby into the pouring rain and watched the water soak right through the cardboard box. On the bright side, the raindrops camouflaged the tears that streaked my face. I ducked under the nearest awning and set the box down to call Andrew.

"Call me when you get this, please. We obviously need to talk. Today was horrendous and all I want right now is a full glass of wine and a foot massage."

I couldn't hail a cab with my arms full which meant I had to take the subway. Also not easy when carrying a box. Even worse, the subway had the stench of dampness. I hated going underground when it rained, but there was no choice. Under the circumstances, I wasn't about to walk thirty-six blocks.

When I finally arrived at the apartment building, I noticed the doorman flinch when he spotted me. Odd. I usually had a nice chat with James at the end of the day. Or

Terrence. Maybe Marc. Whatever his name was, he seemed to like me well enough, so his reaction upon seeing me was strange.

"Everything good?" I asked.

"Cold one today, huh?" he said, pretending to shiver. "I'm looking forward to spring weather."

"You and me both," I said. I trudged past him and through the lobby to the elevator. It was a pre-war building with all the beauty and embellishments of the era's architecture. Unfortunately, that also meant a pre-war elevator. It crawled to the fourth floor and I took the opportunity to dig through my purse for the key. I had a habit of misplacing things, including keys and security cards. I'd lost my security card no fewer than a dozen times during my tenure.

Well, that wouldn't be an issue anymore.

I discovered the key at the bottom of my purse and felt victorious as I attempted to slide the serrated edge into the lock.

Except it didn't fit.

Frowning, I tried again but no dice. I knew it was the right key because it was attached to the Tiffany keyring that Andrew had given to me last year as a gift. Okay, technically, it wasn't a gift. He'd received it from his boss and thought it was too feminine, so he'd passed it along to me. Still, I hadn't paid for it and Andrew had given it to me so it qualified as a gift in my mind.

I looked up and down the hallway to see if the super happened to be within shouting distance. No such luck. I pulled out my phone and looked up his number in my contacts.

"Benito here," he answered.

"Hi, this is Mia Thorne from 4G. My key doesn't seem to be working."

"That's because I changed the locks like you asked me to," he said.

"I didn't ask you to change the locks."

"Mr. Kilkenny told me."

I wasn't sure why he would do that without telling me. "Can you bring me a spare key, please? Andrew didn't tell me anything about this."

"I'm afraid I can't do that."

"Then have someone else do it. I need to get inside. I'm drenched and I've had a terrible day."

He hesitated. "No, ma'am. I mean I'm not allowed to let you in."

I stared at the lock like I might blow it up with laser vision. "What do you mean you're not allowed?"

"Mr. Kilkenny instructed me not to let anyone to have a new key."

"Anyone as in me?"

He cleared his throat. "Yes, ma'am."

My legs nearly slid out from under me. "I don't understand."

"You haven't spoken to Mr. Kilkenny?"

"Clearly not about this or we wouldn't be having this conversation."

"I'm sorry, Miss Thorne. I was under the impression that he would be sharing this information with you today."

"I called him several times to tell him I lost my job, but he hasn't answered."

"You lost your job, too?" Benito interrupted. "Oh, man. Talk about a bad day."

"Yes, it is a no-good, horrible, very bad day." I pressed a shoulder against the wall to keep myself from plummeting to the floor. "When did he give you instructions to install a new lock?"

"When?" Benito asked, clearly stalling.

"Was it today?" Had my proposal somehow sent him spinning into survival mode?

"No, ma'am. It was last week."

Last week. This must've been what Andrew had intended to discuss with me over coffee today. I'd been planning a proposal while he'd been planning a breakup.

"What about my things?" I asked.

"All your stuff's in storage," he said. "It's perfectly safe there until you've made arrangements to move it. Mr. Kilkenny agreed to pay any fees."

"How generous," I said, my tone laced with sarcasm.

I staggered back to the elevator and returned to the lobby where the doorman awaited me. He must've been watching me on the surveillance camera because his expression was pure sympathy.

"I'm sorry," he said. "I wanted to say something, but it wasn't my place."

"It's not your fault," I said, my voice barely a whisper. I had nowhere to go. No job. No home.

"If it's any consolation, she's not nearly as pretty as you are," he said.

My face must have registered surprise because the doorman backed away slowly. "I thought he might have told you by now."

"He hasn't told me anything." There was already a she. A replacement model. How could Andrew have kept this to himself? How were we still living together when there was already another woman in the picture?

"He's a tool, Miss Thorne. A complete tool. You can do better."

I stared at the doorman, tears obscuring my view of him. I was a forty-two-year-old disaster.

"No, Mr. Doorman. I don't think I can."

CHAPTER TWO

I SAT in the Starbucks on 86th and Columbus and tried to put on a brave face. I'd gone from privileged middle-aged white woman in a relationship to unemployed, alone, and homeless in a matter of hours. I didn't even get to fully enjoy the fruits of my flash mob labor.

I sucked down the last of my vanilla soy latte with one extra pump and stared at my phone. As much as I dreaded it, I was going to have to bite the bullet and call my mother. I would've preferred to call my dad, but that would require a direct line to the afterlife since he died when I was twelve. My mother and I weren't exactly close. She was on her third husband and I'd only met the latest one a handful of times, including their wedding. Madeline and Jurgen now lived in Cherry Hill, New Jersey, a place filled with strip malls and highway jughandles I'd successfully managed to avoid visiting, although I feared that would have to change now.

My mother picked up on the first ring. "What's wrong, Mia?"

"What makes you think something's wrong?"

"You're calling me at dinnertime. You never call me between the hours of six and eight."

"That's because I never call you."

"Hence the other reason I know there's a problem. What is it this time? Did your car get towed again? I warned you to stop parking it on the street. You can rent a spot…"

"I lost my job," I blurted. I didn't have the heart to tell her that I'd sold my car two years ago to pay bills. That was before I'd moved in with Andrew. He'd seemed like a white knight in a starched shirt and pleated trousers, riding to my financial rescue.

"Oh, sweetheart. That's terrible. What did you do?"

I held my breath. Naturally she would assume I did something to deserve it. That was the way her brain worked—usually because I'd done something to deserve it.

"There's more," I said. "Andrew has gotten involved with someone else and he kicked me out of the apartment." I didn't mention the flash mob proposal. That would only add insult to injury.

"You're kidding," my mother said. "So much for the packet of perfume samples I sent you."

"That's okay. I still have the last fifty samples you sent me." My mother was constantly sending me makeup and perfume samples that she got for free from her job. I kept a handful in my purse in lieu of pepper spray.

"I told you to sign a contract with that man," she said.

I sighed and pinched the bridge of my nose. "This really isn't the time for I-told-you-so."

"I'm surprised you didn't see these things coming."

I rolled my eyes. "Here we go again."

"Your father used to insist you have a gift." Her tone was mildly mocking. My father used to say I had the family gift, which my mother had always made clear was complete nonsense.

"The only gift I have is the one for bad timing." Okay, maybe I seemed to know things sometimes or I'd get vibes about people, but nothing earth-shattering. I certainly should've foreseen today's cataclysmic events.

"I can't argue with that," my mother said. "In any case, there's a lesson to be learned here."

"Mom, I just told you I'm unemployed and homeless. Can the lesson be learned later?"

"Mia, you're an adult. When is later for a woman your age?"

A woman my age. "How about next Tuesday at three o'clock? I think there's room in my schedule now." Despite my snarky reply, the question stung. "I'm sure I can stay with Tracy for a few nights, but she's got the kids, so it's not a long-term solution."

Tracy Gladstone was a friend from one of my previous jobs who'd actually stuck around after I got fired, probably because she left to become a stay-at-home mom soon after. Most colleagues didn't keep in touch once I left. Then again, I wasn't very good at maintaining relationships. Tracy made an effort and that was the real reason we were still in contact. I'd texted her on my way to Starbucks but didn't expect to hear from her until later. Her kids were involved in all manner of after-school activities and she didn't have a lot of spare time once the school day finished. Watching Tracy constantly have to fire on all cylinders no matter her mood was one of the reasons I'd avoided the topic of kids with Andrew and my boyfriends before him. The thought of setting my own feelings aside and forging ahead for the sake of someone else wasn't in my wheelhouse. I'd once tried to lecture Tracy about the idea of learned helplessness, but she'd pointed out that her children were five and seven and were, in fact, relatively helpless.

"Why don't you go check out that house that your father's

aunt left you?" my mother asked. "It's been sitting empty for months."

I tapped the side of my empty cup. "Um, what house?"

"The one in Pennsylvania near the river."

"I don't know anything about that."

My mother offered her characteristic huff of annoyance. "You would if you ever bothered to read my text messages. I reminded you a month ago. I have the receipts to prove it."

I rolled my eyes. "You're not a Real Housewife, Mom. You don't need to bring the receipts." I paused. "Did she really leave me a whole house?"

"I doubt it's even half of one. I'm sure it's a shack, but it's probably bigger than your apartment and it's certainly better than being homeless. I mean, what would I tell my friends if you had to move in with me at your age?"

"Yes, that's the real concern here. Not that I'd have to pee in a stairwell under the cloak of darkness, but what ever will you tell Maude and Kathleen?"

"I don't know anyone called Maude, and Kathleen was the name of the housecleaner we had when you were a teenager."

"Kathleen was the one you fired because she ate your biscotti."

My mother made a disgruntled noise. "I am not going through this with you again, Mia. It was theft, pure and simple."

"Maybe she was starving because she made less than minimum wage and could barely afford to feed herself."

"Then I doubt a cinnamon biscotti was the answer to her problems."

I wasn't in the mood to argue, not with my life in its current state of unwelcome flux. "Where is this alleged house?"

"A town called Newberry. I've never been there, so I can't tell you more than that. That's what the internet is for."

I tried to recall the name of my father's aunt. It had been many years since she'd been mentioned. "Her name was Hazel Thorne?"

"Yes, she was the younger sister of your father's father."

"Holy smokes, how old was she?"

"I'm not sure exactly. Old. She never married. With your father dead, she had no heirs except you."

"So she didn't leave the house to me specifically," I said. "I was just the only option."

"I'm sure she didn't have to leave it to family if she didn't want to," my mother said. "She could have left it to the SPCA like our old neighbor did. Remember that uproar?" She laughed at the memory. "Each one of those nieces thought they would inherit. I'll give Sheila credit. She had those girls catering to her every whim up until she died."

"It was manipulative if you ask me. Sheila had no intention of leaving her nieces anything."

"That's not true. She left them her jewelry, remember?"

"It was hardly the blue diamond from *Titanic*." My thoughts turned back to my own predicament. "Do you think if I turn up in Newberry, then someone will just hand me the keys to Aunt Hazel's house?"

"I'm sure you'll have papers to sign, but yes. Pretty much. At this point, they'll probably roll out a red carpet. I dread to think of the state of the house now that it's been sitting empty for months. You have a way of letting things fester."

I glanced at the busy street outside. The honking horns and the bustling commuters. Lynette's threat to blackball me. As much as I loved the city, maybe a change was in order—at least in the short-term.

"Fine. I'll go," I said. "But I'm only staying long enough to shower and sell the house. Then I'll figure out next steps."

"Do you need me to resend the text with the information?" my mother asked. I could tell she was trying not to sound too delighted by my acquiescence.

"Would you mind? I'm hopeless with the search function on my phone." And even more hopeless when I knew I'd deleted her messages without reading them.

"I think you should consider staying there. A new start in a new town is a great opportunity. I bet there will be more than a few divorced men. And Jurgen and I can come visit as soon as you're settled. It will be a nice change not to have to stay in a hotel."

I never invited my mother to visit me in the city. She would announce her intentions only days beforehand and swoop into town, expecting me to drop everything to cater to her. My saving grace was the small size of apartments in the city. She had no choice but to book a hotel room.

"I never liked Andrew," she continued. "To begin with, he was cheap and a man should never be cheap, at least not in the early days of courtship."

"This isn't the 1800s, Mom. Nobody's courting anyone."

"You're better off without him. That's all I'm saying."

"Then you and the doorman are in agreement." I didn't want to talk about Andrew or anything else. I felt emotionally drained and my mother would beat this to death if I let her. I waited for the bus to stop outside, knowing the loud hydraulic system would drown out anything else I said. "Thanks for the talk, Mom. Gotta go," I yelled.

I set down the phone and saw the incoming text from my mother—or Nurse Ratched as she was labeled in my contacts. I tapped the screen and reviewed the message and then immediately went to the map app to find Newberry, Pennsylvania. There was no connection by train, but I could take Amtrak or New Jersey Transit as far as Princeton and then take an Uber across the Delaware River from there. I wasn't so broke that I couldn't afford the train ticket and the thirty-minute drive. I could claim the house long enough to put it on the market and sell it, then use the money to tide me over until I began the next phase of my life. Maybe I'd have a mid-life crisis. Blow the money on a fast car and make poor decisions. Hmm. It seemed like my entire adulthood had been one prolonged mid-life crisis, minus the car.

How much did a Maserati cost these days? I quickly dismissed the thought. My mother assumed the house was a shack and I had no reason to doubt her theory. By all accounts, Aunt Hazel had been an odd duck and it was unlikely she'd left a mansion behind. A momentary sadness settled over me. Aunt Hazel had arguably been a lost opportunity. A connection to my father. I recalled years ago when I first learned of the older woman's existence, asking my mother to visit her.

"We're not visiting someone we don't even know," she'd said.

"But she's family," I'd protested.

"In name only," had been her response. "For all we know, she could be a serial killer."

"Have you ever met her?"

My mother had appeared thoughtful, but I knew she remembered. She mentally catalogued every slight, grudge, and grievance, probably listed them in order of severity too.

"She came to our wedding and she sent a gift when you were born."

I'd perked up. "What kind of gift?"

She'd wrinkled her nose. "Something inappropriate."

"A strip-o-gram?"

My mother had sighed deeply. "I believe it was a pack of tarot cards. I gave them away after your father died. You know I don't go in for that sort of thing."

I'd agreed that tarot cards seemed a bizarre choice for the birth of a baby. Still, Hazel Thorne had been the only member left on my father's side of the family. It would've been nice to have had that connection to him, no matter how odd she was.

Too late now.

I closed the app and leaned against the chair. "Looks like I'm finally paying a visit to the mysterious Aunt Hazel, a few months too late."

CHAPTER THREE

THE TOWN of Newberry looked like an artists' colony from the 1800's blended with the West Village in New York City. Psychics, tattoo parlors, a theatre, boutique hotels, and trendy shops and restaurants along cobblestoned paths lined the riverfront. A bridge with a pedestrian walkway spanned the Delaware River, connecting Pennsylvania to New Jersey.

I wandered along the main street, taking in the sights while I searched for the real estate office of Stella Battenberg. I passed a black cannon that, according to the plaque, had been used during the Civil War. I'd never paid much attention to the historical aspects of the city. My knowledge was limited to pre-war versus modern architecture.

I stopped in front of a charming white building with black shutters. This was the address Stella had given me. I opened the door and entered the office. A red-haired woman with glasses on a chain around her neck stood at a desk rifling through papers. She couldn't have been more than five feet tall. Her leopard-print knitwear hugged her ample bosom. It was only when she looked up at me that I saw the evidence of age. If I was a betting woman, I'd put her at seventy-two. The bright red lipstick didn't help either, bless her.

"Are you Stella?"

The older woman lifted the glasses to the bridge of her nose and examined me from head to toe. "Amelia Thorne?"

"Yes, but everyone calls me Mia," I said.

"Welcome to Newberry, Mia." She bustled around the corner of the desk to greet me. "I am so, so sorry about your aunt. Hazel was a dear friend and I miss her terribly."

I wanted to respond in kind, but I didn't know my aunt at all, not that I was above a white lie. Or a bald-faced one. Lying was basically a tool in my survival kit and I didn't hesitate to use it when the situation required it. I'd had a lot of experience as a salesperson.

No, Mr. Turner. Your ad will definitely be in the most prominent position.

Yes, Mrs. Blake, you are absolutely paying less than your direct competitors.

Don't tell the others, but you're my favorite client!

"I'm sorry it took me so long to reply to you, but I only learned about your letter recently," I said.

"Your aunt didn't have a current address for you, so I sent it to your mother and hoped for the best."

"I was living with my boyfriend and it's his apartment..." I trailed off, not wanting to discuss Andrew. At all. Ever again. "This town is cute. I've never been here before."

"I've lived here my whole life," Stella said. "Can't imagine being anywhere else, really."

"I've been in the city most of my adult life, but I moved around a lot," I said.

"Philadelphia?" she asked.

"New York."

"Oh. Hazel disliked cities. The energy was too intense for

her." She gave me a sidelong glance. "I'm surprised you didn't have the same reaction."

That was a strange statement. "I'm used to it, I guess."

Stella peered at me. "You don't mind crowds?"

"They're not my favorite thing in the world, but I've never given it much thought. It's the city, you know?" I was prone to migraines, but I chalked that up to the city noises and hormones.

"Well, you must be excited to take a look at your new home."

It would do in a pinch, but I wasn't looking to settle here. Despite Lynette's threats, I figured she'd forget about me soon enough and I could start the job hunt with money in the bank. It would be a nice change of pace to take my time and not rush into the next role.

"I'm definitely curious," I said.

"Come on, I'll drive." Stella grabbed the handle of a shiny black purse and motioned for me to follow her outside. She teetered along the sidewalk in her heels and I worried she'd break her neck on the uneven pavement. Her car was a white Volkswagen Beetle with *Stella Realty* emblazoned across the side.

I climbed into the passenger seat and watched as the petite woman settled on top of a pink yoga block so she could see over the steering wheel.

The drive was not what I would call relaxing. She jerked to a stop at the end of every block, subjecting me to whiplash, and she nearly mowed down a couple crossing the road.

"Ten points for the one wearing the socks with sandals," she said with a raspy cackle that threatened to morph into a cough. She revved the engine and for a moment I actually believed she intended to hit the gas. I mean, I agreed with her about the socks and sandals, but I wasn't sure that a hit-and-run was the answer.

She continued to drive along a narrow, curvy road and kept removing her hands from the steering wheel to gesture as she talked. Part of me wanted to grab her hands and glue them back to the wheel. By the time she pulled into a pebbled driveway, I thought I might be sick.

"Welcome to Red Clover," Stella announced.

"Wait. The house has a name?" I peered through the windshield for a better view. It wasn't exactly Downton Abbey, but I had to admit there was a certain charm to the bright yellow house with its black door, black shutters, and overgrown window boxes. It also featured a pitched gabled roof with two dormers and a large chimney.

"It looks like a fairytale cottage," I said, "but why is it called Red Clover when the house is yellow?"

Stella scrunched her nose in a way that suggested I'd asked a stupid question. "That's not yellow. That's marigold. And red clover is a type of flower." She looked at me askance. "Don't you know anything about flowers?"

"I know that the cost of roses increases exponentially around Valentine's Day and poinsettias are poisonous. Does that count?"

Stella gave me a strange look as she exited the car and I followed her to the front door. The older woman rummaged through her black purse for the key.

"As you can see the outside has gotten a little untidy in the months following Hazel's death, but I'm sure you can turn that around quickly."

I barked a laugh. "If you knew me, you'd understand why that's funny."

"I don't suppose you had to deal with a large yard, living in the city." Stella finally produced a key and unlocked the door.

"I've never had to deal with a yard of any size," I said. The extent of my time outside revolved around outdoor cafes and rooftop parties. "It's too much responsibility anyway."

Stella offered an uneasy smile. "I see." She entered the house and immediately stepped aside to give me space. "So, first impressions?"

Wispy spiderwebs clung to the beamed ceiling. Despite the size and spaciousness of the room, I almost failed to spot the wooden floors because they were covered with random pieces of furniture and throw rugs.

"Well, Aunt Hazel and I have clutter in common," I remarked.

"I've been coming here to feed Ophelia, taking turns with Gladys and a couple other folks."

"Who's Ophelia?" I asked.

Stella's gaze swept the interior of the house. "That's Ophelia," she said, pointing to a deep window seat where an overweight black and white cat licked her paws.

"Hard to miss her. What kind of cat is she?"

"Tuxedo," Stella said. "Don't you know anything about cats?"

"You can go away and leave them for a weekend without needing to hire a pet sitter," I said. At least that's what I'd gleaned from cat-having friends in the city.

Ophelia seemed to realize that she was the subject of conversation and raised her head to regard us. I took a step toward her and she hissed violently before jumping to the floor with a thud and running away.

"I'm surprised she didn't dent the floor when she landed," I said. Ophelia was surprisingly graceful for a cat that must've weighed twenty pounds.

"She comes with the house, so I hope you're not allergic," Stella said.

"I don't know. I've never had a cat." Or any pet, for that

matter. My mother was firmly in the no-pet camp and then I moved to the city as an adult where it was easier to find an apartment without an animal in tow.

"You've got Hazel's blood. I'm sure you two will get along swimmingly," Stella said, although the crease in her brow undermined her confident declaration.

Based on her size, it seemed likely that Ophelia ate anyone she disliked. I made a mental note to research cat treats. My knowledge of a cat's favorite foods came from *Tom and Jerry* and I wasn't sure how reliable the information was.

We continued the tour of the house and I sneezed a few times from the dust. Would it have killed them to bring a duster along when they came to feed the cat?

The kitchen had a deep farmhouse sink, white cabinets, and butcher block countertops. Pots and pans hung from a ceiling fixture above our heads. A floral scent lingered in the air, though I couldn't identify it.

Stella stared down at the floor. "Oh, the bowls are empty. Oops. I must've missed my turn." She promptly filled the water bowl and placed it back on the floor. "You'll find the walk-in pantry big enough to store all your supplies."

The moment she opened the door, the smell of herbs and spices assaulted my senses. Jars and containers were crammed onto the shelves. I'd like to say that each item was labeled and organized by type or color or *something*, but the chaos that reigned throughout the house was evident in the pantry as well.

Stella opened a bag of cat kibble and retreated from the pantry to dump a cupful into the second bowl.

"Was she a prepper?" I asked.

Stella laughed. "She wasn't planning to ride out the apocalypse in her bunker, if that's what you mean."

"Why did she keep all this stuff?"

"She used it," Stella said.

"To what? Make potpourri?" There were more dried herbs and flowers in this small space than I'd seen in my lifetime.

"Why don't you take a look at the upstairs?" Stella suggested. "I'll wait for you down here."

The older woman was either too infirm or too unsteady on her heels to walk up the steps. It was fine; I didn't need an escort to check out the three bedrooms. The master bedroom was surprisingly large but built into the eaves so the walls were slanted. I had no doubt I'd hit my head every morning when I got out of bed. The sliding barn door was a cool feature, though. The master bathroom had a separate shower and a claw-foot tub surrounded by candles. It seemed that Hazel enjoyed a relaxing bubble bath after a long, hard day of making potpourri.

I returned to the main floor to find Stella waiting by the kitchen door. "The pipes are noisy and the plumbing doesn't like it when you use too much toilet paper, but you'll figure out all the little quirks."

"Is there a handyman you can recommend?"

Stella surveyed the space around me. "What? You see something broken?"

"Not specifically, but a place like this probably has a hundred little jobs that need doing."

"I'll text you a list. I'm sure you're eager to see outside. There's so much to appreciate." She appeared to balance on two popsicle sticks as she made her way out of the house.

We started on the deck that overlooked the river. Ophelia was stretched out across the boards in a patch of sunlight.

"How did she get out here?" I asked.

"She has her own door," Stella explained. "She spends a lot of time outside."

"She doesn't run away?"

Stella seemed taken aback by the question. "Why would she do that? This is her home."

"The deck is nice," I said. "I've always wanted an outdoor space for entertaining." Gazing at the peaceful scenery around me, I momentarily forgot my plan to cut and run.

"You could put heat lamps out here and use it all year round," Stella suggested. "Hazel didn't bother. She spent most of her time in the garden anyway."

"I'd probably do the opposite," I said.

"There's a shed as well as a small barn on the property," Stella said. "I can show you both."

"Are they scary?" I asked, feeling uneasy. I didn't even like going to the basement of my apartment building to do laundry. I didn't want to end up with my head in a dryer and the rest of me in the washing machine.

Stella took her time descending the two steps of the deck. "Hazel used them for storage."

Okay, that didn't really answer my question.

I surveyed the yard and saw nothing except overgrown bushes and weeds. It was like an English garden on testosterone.

"Is everything dead?" I asked.

Stella pursed her lips. "It was the strangest thing. The garden seemed to stop thriving the moment Hazel passed away, like it knew."

"I may not know much about plants, but I'm pretty sure that's not how they work."

We walked along a dirt path that cut straight through two of the gardens. I brushed too close to a bush and my coat got caught on the thorns.

"Don't pull too hard," Stella warned. "These bloom into beautiful roses. You don't want to ruin them."

I extracted myself from the bush, careful not to let the thorns scratch my hand in the process.

"It's nice to be so close to the water," I said. I gazed across the Delaware River to the line of trees. "Is it safe to be this close to New Jersey, though? We don't need hazmat suits or anything?"

"You can't catch an STD from this distance," Stella said in a tone that suggested she'd tested the theory.

She guided me to the shed and the small barn that, thankfully, sheltered only objects and no animals. One cat was enough.

"This must be for clutter overflow," I said.

"You could have quite a yard sale when the weather improves."

But was any of it worth selling? It seemed like junk, as my mother would say.

"You can explore more later," Stella said. "We need to get moving. I made you an appointment with the lawyer to get the paperwork signed."

"Oh, I didn't realize."

We headed toward the main house. As we passed by the thorny bush again, I edged away so I didn't get caught. It was then that I spotted a single red rose. How had I missed it before?

"Isn't it early for the roses to bloom?" I asked.

Stella's stunned expression seemed to answer my question. "That flower wasn't there before, hon."

"I'm sure it was. We probably didn't notice because we were focused on my coat getting snagged."

Stella gave an adamant shake of her head. "No. That rose bloomed in the past twenty minutes. I'd swear to it."

"Weird," I said, not giving it a second thought. I continued toward the house, eager to finish the tour and sign whatever paperwork awaited me.

"What do you think?" Stella asked, as we approached the house.

"I'm sure there's a landscape business that would love to get its hands on this yard."

"I don't know about that," Stella said. "Hazel didn't like anyone messing with her garden. She was very particular."

"Well, if I'm going to sell it, I'll need to hire someone to clean it up and show off its potential. No one will want to buy a jungle."

Stella rounded on me. "Sell it? Why on earth would you do a thing like that?"

"Because I don't live here," I said slowly.

"But you can live here now. You have a beautiful property, or at least it will be once you've been here long enough to spread some of that Thorne magic."

"Oh, I don't have any gardening skills. I can't even keep a cactus alive. Believe me, I've tried."

"But you saw what happened to that rose when you touched the bush," she said. "You have to stay."

I laughed. "You think I did that? That rose was probably there the whole time. We just weren't paying close attention."

"Red Clover has been waiting for you," Stella insisted. "You are its rightful owner."

"Aren't you a realtor? You should want to sell so you can make a commission."

"Hazel intended for *you* to live here," Stella said firmly.

"Dead or alive, she can't make me live here against my will," I said.

"You'll have to discuss it with Mr. Fairfax," she said, lifting her chin in defiance.

"Who's Mr. Fairfax?"

"Dane Fairfax, Hazel's lawyer. He has the papers you need to sign."

A hissing sound drew my attention to the ground behind me. Ophelia stood there in the classic Halloween cat pose—back arched and jaw unhinged.

"She seems angry," I said.

"Because you're talking about selling the house," Stella shot back.

"I highly doubt the cat wants me to stay here. She looks ready to eviscerate me with her eyes."

"She recognizes you as Hazel's rightful heir."

"She recognizes me as dinner, more like. I doubt she cares about anyone as long as she's getting fed."

"You'd be surprised." Stella gave the cat a meaningful look. "I swear Ophelia has lived here longer than anyone."

If anyone would know, it was the vampiric realtor.

Stella's phone pinged. "Oops. That's the alarm. We'd better get moving. Mr. Fairfax will be expecting you."

As we returned to the car, I wondered whether she was sweet on this Mr. Fairfax. Stella wasn't wearing a wedding ring. Maybe she and the lawyer had a little fling going. Good for her.

"I'll drop you off and Mr. Fairfax offered to drive you back here afterward."

"You're not staying?"

"Sorry, I have a showing." The tires squealed as she backed out of the driveway, spraying pebbles in all directions. "Don't worry, though. He's a sweetheart and an excellent lawyer."

At this point, I was more concerned with whether he was a better driver so I could return to Red Clover in one piece.

CHAPTER FOUR

THE LAWYER'S office was located at the north end of the main street, before the break between the residential and commercial sections. According to the plaque, the historic house was built in 1790 and later converted for professional use. The Law Office of Dane Fairfax took up the main floor and a small engineering firm occupied the second floor. Talk about the most boring building in town.

There was no sign of an assistant, so I wandered from room to room until I found someone. The wooden floor squeaked with every step. I was glad I didn't work here; that sound would drive me insane.

The lawyer stood with his back to the doorway, swearing at a printer. I had to admit, I was impressed with his creative curses.

I cleared my throat to get his attention. The lawyer swung around, appearing mortified to see a witness to his frustration. Wow. I was not expecting…him. With dark blonde hair and blue eyes that pierced my very soul, he was younger and more attractive than I expected. Scratch that. He was flat-out hot. Like Matthew McConaughey hot but taller and without the Texas twang.

"I am so sorry," he said, adjusting his blue tie. "My assistant is out today and the printer has decided to throw a fit."

"Seems like the printer's not the only one," I said, smiling.

"Dane Fairfax," he said, and shook my hand. I was a respectable five-foot-seven yet he towered over me. "Let's just say I should leave the fixing of the printer to the professionals. Never, ever stick your hand somewhere it doesn't belong."

"Good advice for all occasions," I quipped. "I'm Mia Thorne. Stella said you have papers I need to sign."

"I do. Give me one minute. They're on my desk."

This guy looked more like an actor playing a lawyer on American television. I specified American TV because I'd seen a few British shows and their fake lawyers looked more like the guy who worked at the deli in my last neighborhood. Far too ordinary to fill my screen. Andrew called them 'character actors,' but I didn't care. I felt cheated, like I'd paid for a chili cheese dog and received a breakfast sausage link in its place.

"I'm sorry about your aunt," Dane said, quickly organizing the papers on his desk. "I didn't know her well, but I enjoyed her company. Legal documents can be boring, as I'm sure you can imagine, but Hazel always found a way to liven up our meetings."

I smiled. "Sounds like Hazel and I have that in common."

"This won't take long, unless you want to go over it with a fine-tooth comb. It's only a few documents."

"I'm not sure it matters what they say," I told him. "I'm signing on the dotted line regardless."

"I would think you'd want to know the details," he said.

"Stella said you'd be able to drop me at the house afterward," I said. It wasn't actually too far to walk, but there was no sidewalk along River Road and it would be an excuse to get to know Mr. Fairfax a little better. There was no sign of a ring, not that its absence was conclusive. I knew plenty of men who eschewed a wedding band.

Dane rifled through a few pages and paused. "Oh, and there's a letter for you in the file." He produced a standard envelope from the folder on his desk and passed it to me. "Don't feel like you need to read it now if you'd like privacy."

I stared at the envelope addressed to me in neat script. "Hazel wrote this?"

"Yes, she wanted you to receive it upon her death."

It felt odd to hold an envelope addressed to me from a relative I'd never met. What could Aunt Hazel possibly have known about me apart from my name and the fact that I existed?

"Are you okay, Miss Thorne? It is Miss, isn't it?"

I shifted in my seat, realizing that my expression must've matched the strange swirl of emotions I felt inside.

"Yes, fine. Sorry, this is all kind of a shock. It's a relief that Stella is so organized. I don't think I would've known what to do."

"Stella is a gem." Dane flashed a brilliant smile that suggested expensive dental work. Whatever he had done, it was worth it. Those teeth could entice even the most resistant people into the orthodontist's chair.

"How old is she?" I asked.

"Ageless. If it weren't for the fact that she works during daylight hours, I'd say she's a vampire."

"Omigod, I had the same thought," I said.

"The estate includes Red Clover and all its contents, as well as its two acres. You should be aware that the property is located in a flood zone, but Stella can help you with the insurance you'll need for that."

"I'll leave that to the new owner," I said.

Dane chuckled. "You are the new owner, Miss Thorne. That's why you're here."

"I am today, but I'm planning to put it on the market as soon as I have it cleaned up."

He frowned. "I'm afraid it's not that simple."

"Oh, I know. I saw the gardens. They're straight out of a horror movie, like a fragrant and slightly more attractive corn maze."

Dane seemed to smile despite himself. "There's a provision you might want to note…" He flipped through the document until he found what he was looking for. "You can only take full possession of Red Clover if you agree to live there for twelve months. Should you live elsewhere or attempt to sell the house within that time, the will is deemed null and void."

I leaned forward with my jaw hanging open. "You can't be serious."

"I'm afraid I am, most of the time. It may surprise you to learn that people don't want their lawyers to be comedians."

I stared at the document in disbelief. Aunt Hazel was a wily one; I'd give her that. "Twelve months," I murmured.

Dane smiled. "It's not so bad. I happen to really like Newberry, though I may be biased since I've never lived anywhere else, except Philadelphia."

"For college?"

"And law school. I spent seven years total at Penn. Came home plenty during that time, though. I didn't like to stay away for long."

It seemed like an alien concept to me. I'd never had a home that felt like…home.

"I guess I don't have much of a choice."

"You're not prevented from going to the city, if that's where your friends are." He hesitated. "Maybe a boyfriend."

"Not anymore," I said, scowling. Did Dane seem...relieved?

"You should get to know the town a little. There will be a decent crowd at Jama this weekend," he said.

"What's Jama?"

"Cuban bar and restaurant. There's a big outdoor porch with heat lamps this time of year to keep you warm. You can't miss it. Both the food and drinks are fantastic."

"I am easily persuaded by mojitos," I said, mulling it over. "Will you be there?"

"I don't tend to..." He stopped mid-sentence. "My brother's always giving me a hard time about getting out more."

"Your brother, huh? You're not twins, are you?" That image would be enough to fuel my fantasies through another winter.

"No, Derek's two years younger than I am."

I could work with that. "Do you get along or are you like those brothers that revert to adolescence when you're together and wrestle each other to the ground?"

"We fall somewhere in the middle of that description," he said.

I was mildly disappointed. I wouldn't mind watching a Fairfax brother wrestling match.

"Is there a car, by any chance?" I asked. Preferably a fast one with two seats and a convertible top.

The lawyer appeared confused. "A car?"

"She had a house to pass down to me. Did she also have a car? I didn't see one."

"Oh, I see. No, Hazel stopped driving a few years ago. Her eyesight was failing."

"That's too bad." Still, it seemed like I'd be able to get around town easily enough and there was always the internet for shopping.

"I'm sorry if the provision disrupted your plans," Dane said.

I waved him off. "I've found that life is nothing but a series of reactions to surprises."

He smiled again and my body warmed in response. "On that note, what do you say, Miss Thorne? How are you going to react to the surprise of Newberry? Are you going to give us a chance?"

How could I resist when the question was being asked by Matthew McConaufairfax? I held out my hand for a pen.

"Where do I sign?"

The hot lawyer delivered me safely to Red Clover in his gunmetal grey Range Rover. The ride was as smooth as his skin and I definitely felt a blast of heat between us as we sat side-by-side. Or maybe it was a hot flash. Sometimes it was hard to tell the difference.

He turned off the car and opened the door.

"You're coming?" I asked, surprised.

He hesitated. "I thought I would walk you to the door."

I laughed. "It's not a date." I immediately regretted my response. I was more than happy to let a ridiculously handsome man walk me to the door, date or no date.

He stiffened. "No, of course not." He closed his door and I longed to undo the past sixty seconds. "Let me know if you have any questions. You have my card."

"And you know where I live," I joked. I fled the car before I said anything else.

I unlocked the front door with caution, hoping the cat wasn't lurking in the shadows and waiting to attack me in order to suck out my soul. I stood in the center of the living room and did a slow, complete turn. This place was going to be my home for the next twelve months. A sense of calm washed over me and I chalked it up to exhaustion. I was rarely calm. My anxiety meant that I spent most of my time on edge, waiting to see if I landed a new client, or what my mother wanted to complain about this time, or whether the latest boyfriend was in the relationship for the long-haul (newsflash: they never were). Red Clover, however, seemed like a safe haven. A bubble from the outside world.

I returned to the kitchen for a drink and spotted the envelope on the counter addressed to me. No time like the present. I tore open the envelope and removed the letter from Aunt Hazel.

The sharp ring of the doorbell startled me and I jumped forward, knocking my shin against the doorjamb. That would be a bruise by morning. I dropped the letter on the counter and hopped on one foot to the front door to see who'd interrupted my peaceful moment.

The woman on the doorstep was no taller than five-foot-three with dark hair cut chin-length and dyed blue at the tips. Her almond-shaped eyes were like two pools of ink. The man loomed over her at about six feet. With his chiseled features and deep brown eyes, he looked like a catalogue model, except for the shaggy coat he wore. He was like the Sears version of Liberace.

"I'm not interested," I said flatly.

"But you don't even know why we're here," the woman said, seemingly perplexed.

The man nudged his companion. "I like her already."

"Trust me. I don't buy leggings or off-brand makeup and your religion doesn't want me," I said.

The man's smile grew broader. "Now I really like her."

The woman persevered. "I'm Scarlet York and this is Patrick Beaumont."

"I'm your neighbor, two doors down," Patrick added. His voice was so velvety soft, I wanted to wrap it around me like a blanket. "We just want to introduce ourselves and welcome you to the neighborhood."

"Thank you. I'm Amelia Thorne, but everybody calls me Mia."

Patrick cocked his head. "How is Mia a nickname for Amelia?"

"What do you mean? It has the letters m-i-a right there in the name."

Patrick gave me a sharp look. "So what? Theodore has 'h-o-r-e,' but you didn't hear anyone calling Teddy Roosevelt that."

Scarlet elbowed her friend in the ribs. "I told you to be nice."

Patrick looked affronted. "This is me being nice. I didn't call *her* a whore." He turned back to face me. "It's not real fur, by the way."

"I didn't say it was."

"No, but you had that question in your eyes." His finger zigzagged between my eyes. "You were wondering whether to judge me."

"I've seen enough fake fur in my life, Patrick. You don't need to explain."

"I own a landscaping and nursery business in town," Scarlet interrupted, clearly trying to regain control of the conversation.

"Oh, now I see why you're here. You've probably wanted to get your hands on this garden for years and you see this as your big chance."

Scarlet offered a shy smile. "I used to beg Hazel to help with her garden. It's a masterpiece. She didn't like anyone else to touch it, though. I thought as she got older, she would find the work harder, but she never did."

"So you're not to blame for the monstrosity outside?" I asked.

"I would've loved to tackle it, but my hands were tied. I guess you're the niece."

"She was my father's aunt," I said. "I never knew her."

"Oh, that's a shame," Scarlet said. "Everyone liked Hazel."

"Not everyone," Patrick said. "It would be weird if everyone liked her. That's not normal."

"Neither are you," Scarlet said under breath.

"Do you want to come in?" It felt odd to invite strangers into my house. I would never have done that in the city. I didn't even like standing too close to someone in an elevator.

"Don't mind if I do," Patrick said, stepping past me. "Where are you from?"

"New York."

Patrick clapped his hands together. "Love. Have you ever been to…?"

Scarlet cut him off, joining him in the living room. "Let's not play that game right now."

Ophelia chose this moment to make her appearance. The cat stalked across the floor like a hefty lion in pursuit of a gazelle.

"What's she doing?" Patrick asked.

"Don't ask me. I only just met her."

"I bet she's really missing Hazel," Scarlet said. "Those two were inseparable."

"Really?" I twisted to watch the cat as she stopped to attack the fringe of the rug. "She's not the nicest cat in the world. She already tried to bite me."

"Ophelia can be very territorial," Patrick agreed. "It took her years to warm to me."

"It takes everyone years to warm to you," Scarlet said. She turned back to me. "I'll bring you over some catnip."

"I don't need any help sleeping, thanks. I am a champion sleeper."

"Not catnap," Patrick said, shaking his head. "Cat*nip*."

"It helps you bond with your cat, both physically and psychically," Scarlet added.

Psychically? I resisted the urge to roll my eyes. I'd only just met them. I had to keep my sarcasm in check or I'd alienate the only two people interested in getting to know me.

I continued to watch Ophelia as she jumped onto the sofa and dragged her belly across the cushions. "Well, she's not my cat. She belonged to Aunt Hazel."

"Ophelia doesn't belong to anyone," Scarlet said. "She's her own creature. Still, if you're going to be sharing a home with her, catnip is a good idea. Something to get her on your side."

"So catnip is basically the cocktail of the cat world," I said.

Patrick smiled. "Funny you should mention that because Scarlet and I came by to invite you to come out with us. We thought you might like to see the nightlife in Newberry—what there is of it."

"As a matter of fact, someone suggested I go to Jama tonight. Do you know it?"

They exchanged glances. "That wouldn't be my first choice," Patrick said.

"But that sounds great," Scarlet interjected. "Who recommended it?"

"The lawyer who handles Aunt Hazel's estate. Mr. Fairfax."

"Dane Fairfax?" Patrick asked.

"Yes, that's him. He said his brother likes it there."

Patrick snorted. "Yeah, that sounds about right."

Scarlet pressed the heel of her shoe on top of his boot. "We'd be happy to drive you, if you need a ride."

"Really? You don't mind."

"Scarlet loves to drive," Patrick said. "It gives her a false sense of control."

"I prefer the back of a cab. Just tell the driver where to drop me and sit back and relax."

"Do you have any questions about the town or the house?" Scarlet asked. "If you need your own local Alexa, I'm willing."

"Alexa is a pervy stalker as far as I'm concerned, eavesdropping on my conversations and always telling me to have a good day. Who does that?"

"Sounds like my mother," Patrick said.

"Okay, then I'll be your local tour guide. How about that?" Scarlet watched me expectantly.

I eyed her suspiciously. "Why?"

"Because this is a small town and you're new," Scarlet said.

"And you want me to hire you to clean up the gardens," I finished for her. I'd wooed enough clients to understand her strategy.

"If that happens as a result, great," she said. "If not, then I've made a friend. They're both pretty good outcomes as far as I'm concerned."

To her credit, her response seemed genuine.

"I noticed a weird trashcan outside," I said. "I meant to ask Stella about it, but I got distracted."

We exited out the laundry room door to where the oversized black bin sat.

"This is the compost bin," Scarlet said.

I squinted at the bin with trepidation. "I'm not familiar with the term."

"You put your organic waste in it. The waste breaks down over time and then you can use it for gardening."

I grimaced. "You expect me to put rotten food on my plants." My gaze swept the backyard jungle. "That explains a lot," I whispered to myself.

"I could teach you," Scarlet said. "I offer a variety of services, not just landscaping. Composting is a way of honoring your relationship with the planet."

"I see," I said carefully. I could feel my mother's judgment from here. Madeline Albrecht would've kindly escorted Scarlet off the property by now and dismissed her as a loon.

"Nature was sacred to Hazel and she did everything she could to show respect and maintain an active connection with it." Scarlet smiled to herself. "It was one of the things I really liked about her."

My gaze swept the surrounding area. "I don't know how I'm going to get this garden under control. I don't even know how to identify any of the plants. Unless it's a rose, I'm clueless."

Scarlet clasped her hands in front of her. "That's my specialty don't forget."

Patrick gently smacked her arm. "Enough with the hard sell. You've made your point."

I wanted to offer Scarlet a small reward for her effort, one former salesperson to another.

"Why don't you come by tomorrow and give me advice on where to start?" Or how. Or anything, really.

Scarlet beamed at me. "That sounds great."

"We'll pick you up at nine," Patrick said.

"I'll be ready. Thanks for stopping by." I realized how good it felt to start with a clean slate. No one here knew anything about me or my recent humiliations.

"Oh, by the way," Patrick said. "I love a woman with chutzpah. I don't care what anyone says—a public proposal is always a good idea." He fluffed his fuzzy collar and turned dramatically toward the door.

Scarlet lowered her head meekly. "Sorry you didn't get the answer you wanted," she whispered and ducked out the house.

I closed the door and sagged against it. So much for starting over.

CHAPTER FIVE

I HAD a few hours before I needed to change for Jama, so I inspected every room in the house, opening closet doors with a sample perfume bottle in my hand as I checked for hidden murderers and rapists. Even if I ended up spraying the empty air, the room would smell divine.

Ophelia followed me from room to room, her stomach dragging across the throw rugs and the slats of pine. I was surprised she didn't end up with splinters in her fur. Maybe she did and failed to notice.

It was only when I entered the kitchen to hydrate for tonight that I remembered Aunt Hazel's letter. I glanced at the counter where I'd left it but it wasn't there.

I sighed and looked at the cat. "What did you do with the letter?"

Ophelia meowed and ran away. The movement stirred a sheet of paper on the floor. I scooped it up and read—

Dearest Amelia,

. . .

A shame we never got to meet, but such is the will of the universe. If you're reading this, then my time on earth has come to an end. It's been a good run. No complaints, except for a few minor ones that I won't burden you with...but I really would've preferred a different ending to Game of Thrones. Anyway, I won't trouble you with such trivial matters. The purpose of this letter is to welcome you to Newberry and wish you well in your new life.

I paused. Why was she so certain I'd decide to start a new life here? I could've been happily married and gainfully employed. I set my attitude aside and continued reading.

Ophelia will be a good companion for you. She might not take to you at first, but don't let that put you off. Some of the best relationships take time to cultivate, like some of the best gardens. I hope you will love tending to the gardens of Red Clover as much as I have. Honestly, nothing has brought me as much joy. The most important thing to know, however, is this—

The letter stopped abruptly. I turned it over but the backside was blank. "What the...? The most important thing to know is what?"

I grabbed my phone and looked up the number for the hot lawyer.

Voicemail. Great.

"Um, Mr. Fairfax, this is Mia Thorne. There seems to be a page missing from my aunt's letter and I was hoping you might have it in a file or something. Please call me back and let me know. Thanks."

Talk about a cliffhanger ending. Thanks, Aunt Hazel!

My phone rang and I glimpsed 'Nurse Ratched' on the

screen before I could shut my eyes and feign ignorance to myself. Against my better judgment, I decided to answer it. I needed to complain to someone, so I considered this payback for all the times I had to set the phone down on speaker while my mother droned on about a litany of complaints from the nail color of the cashier at the supermarket to the scratchy wool blend of the socks I bought her for Christmas.

"Hey, Mom."

"Well, it's about time you answered. I was worried you were dead in the canal and no one would find you for so long that they'd have to reconstruct your face to be able to identify you."

"Have you been watching *Bones* reruns again?"

"That's irrelevant."

"Is it?"

"How's the house?" she asked.

"A mess. Well, the house isn't, but the garden is. And her cat should've been put on a diet a decade ago."

"Was she as strange as she seemed?" my mother asked.

"How would I know? I never met her."

"You know what I mean. Are there tarot cards and voodoo dolls everywhere?"

"There's a lot of *stuff*." I hadn't really looked closely enough to notice tarot cards or crystal balls.

"Just as I suspected," she said with a note of triumph.

"Why do you think she was strange?" I asked. "Was it something she said or did?"

"It's hard to remember all the details now, but according to your father, Hazel believed she was psychic and that the ability was passed down in the family through the female line."

"So you're saying my estrogen has psychic powers?"

"I never believed any of it, of course. All that nonsense is for weak-minded individuals."

"What about Dad?"

"What about him?"

"Did he think it was nonsense?" Hazel was his aunt. He must've formed an opinion at some point during their lifetime.

My mother hesitated. "I've told you before. There were a few times when you were a child that he insisted you were more in tune with the world than you should be."

I snorted. "What does that even mean?"

"He seemed to think you knew things, but he never considered that you only knew them because you were involved."

Troublemaker. Rabble rouser. My identity from a young age.

"I remember Stephanie Fitzgibbons' doll."

"Oh, yes. That debacle. What a mess." I could practically hear her eyes roll. "Well, I think the whole thing is silly and I'm glad Hazel never got her claws into you to convince you otherwise. Imagine how much more screwed-up your life would be now."

Ouch. "Gee, thanks for the pep talk."

"Oh, don't be so sensitive, Mia. You know what I mean."

Yes, I knew exactly what she meant. If there was an opportunity to criticize me, my mother seized it with both hands.

"What's the verdict then?" she continued. "Do you think you'll stay?"

"It seems I have to." I explained the rules attached to the inheritance.

"How about that? Your aunt was as clever as she was batty."

"Her lawyer isn't batty and he liked Aunt Hazel. He said she livened things up for him."

"I'm sure she did. That's what a laughingstock does. Do

you want to be a laughingstock, Mia?" She paused. "Don't answer that. Anyone who subjects herself to ridicule the way you do…"

"I didn't intend…"

"The road to hell is paved with good intentions, Mia. You're forty-two-years old. When are you going to act like it? Jurgen thinks you're emotionally stunted because of your father's death. If only I'd put you in therapy like Grandma suggested at the time, God rest her challenging soul."

I winced. "Jurgen hasn't spent any significant time with me, so if that's what he thinks, then he's getting it from you."

"Maybe so, but I think he's right. You need to grow up. Learn how to be a mature woman and then maybe you'll find a real man willing to stick around."

I fought the urge to groan into the phone. There were many reasons I avoided talking to my mother and this common refrain was definitely one of them.

"Aunt Hazel seemed to live a perfectly satisfactory life and she never married."

"Fine then. Have it your way. Don't have children. Be another crazy Hazel that everybody talks about but nobody talks to."

"As it happens, I already have plans tonight," I said, not even bothering to hide my smug tone.

"Oh? Who with?"

"Local people." I wasn't foolish enough to offer any names. That would serve as ammunition she'd use against me at a later point.

She sighed into the phone. "I need to go. Jurgen made reservations at a new sushi restaurant and we can't be late or they'll give away our table."

"We wouldn't want that. I'll talk to you later." Much later.

"Good-bye, Mia. If you accept drinks from strange men, make sure they come directly from the bartender to you."

"It's a miracle I've lived this long without you peering over my shoulder at all times."

I clicked off the phone and set it on the counter. A memory stirred and I leaned my hip against the butcher block, letting the image bubble to the surface. A doll with auburn hair, bright eyes, and a blue dress—Stephanie Fitzgibbons' prized possession. She carried the doll everywhere and her older brothers used to make fun of her until she cried. One day the doll disappeared and the brothers swore up and down they had no knowledge of the doll's whereabouts. Their parents turned their bedrooms upside down in search of the doll and found nothing. When I saw Stephanie in tears that afternoon, an image of the doll had flashed in my mind, along with the fort in the woods. I made the mistake of blurting out the doll's location. The brothers claimed I'd stolen the doll and hid it at the fort to avoid detection. It seemed that was a more plausible explanation and the one everyone chose to believe. Stephanie didn't speak to me after that and I learned to keep my lucky guesses to myself.

I climbed the wooden steps to the bedroom to decide on an outfit for the evening. My suitcase was unzipped on the bed so I flipped it open and scrutinized the options. Newberry was a small town with an artsy vibe. I wasn't sure how my business casual look would fit in. I chose jeans and a knit top with boots. The bar area was outdoors so I'd need an extra layer in case I was too far from a heat lamp.

I glanced in my jewelry roll and spotted a bracelet that Andrew had given me. It was hard enough to believe he'd been seeing someone behind my back to the point where he'd decided to move her into the apartment. If I were being honest with myself, I would acknowledge a few red flags in recent months. But I wasn't in the mood to be honest with myself. I was in the mood to drink and be merry with relative strangers. If I was going to live in Newberry for the next year, it was in my best interest to make friends.

Jama had an inviting outdoor dining area with an attractive wraparound front porch, complete with a huge bar and paddle fans unmoving overhead. Heat lamps were strategically stationed around the porch and I imagined the fans would get a lot of use in a couple months when the summer temperatures set in. A shiny black grand piano was positioned just outside the entrance and there seemed to be enough room for a small band.

"You don't mind drinking outside, do you?" Scarlet asked. "The inside is nice, but I prefer to be outside unless it's raining."

"Sounds good to me," I said. I noticed a trio of men in suits at the bar. For a brief moment, I was back in the city, stopping by a bar after work. I wondered where these three worked that required more than a T-shirt and jeans. Financial services, most likely. Even towns like Newberry needed people to manage money.

"I've got eyes on a pair of broad shoulders," Patrick said under his breath.

I had no idea which pair of broad shoulders he meant. Patrick took the lead and sidled up to the guy on the end.

"Three sarsaparillas, bartender," he said.

The bartender broke into a wide grin when he noticed Patrick. "Hey, haven't seen you here for a bit."

"You know I hibernate in the winter," Patrick said.

"Hey, Scarlet," the bartender said. "Good to see you mingling with civilization."

"It happens on occasion," Scarlet said.

"Pete, I'd like you to meet our new friend, Mia," Patrick said. "She just moved to town."

Pete shook my hand. "Welcome to Newberry." He motioned to the trio of suits. "Do you guys know each other?"

Patrick leaned his elbows on the counter, fully invested in the introduction. "I don't believe so."

"This is Carlton, Leo, and Jax," Pete said. "We all graduated together many moons ago."

"Pays to have a friend who's the local bartender," the man identified as Carlton said.

"Not tonight," Pete said. "You've only had one beer."

"Shouldn't have even had one," Carlton admitted. "Apparently it messes with antibiotics."

Leo jabbed Carlton with an elbow. "Told you not to go to Mexico without taking one of those preventative pills ahead of time."

"Hey, what about me?" Jax said. "I can't even hold my beer with my dominant hand." He held up a bandaged hand. "I'm the only one I know who could get hurt wrestling with office supplies."

I was a sucker for a slightly clumsy but affable guy—basically, Hugh Grant in any movie—although Jax was too short to be my type.

"Jax was the only other guy in gym class likely to trip over his own feet," Pete said. "The two of us would hide behind the bleachers and smoke until it was time to get changed."

Patrick cringed. "Oh, you smoke?"

"Not anymore," Jax said. "That habit died out sometime in college. Too off-putting to the ladies."

Patrick's shoulders sagged. "Yes, the ladies."

"Is there a collective noun for a group of adults who are a complete mess?" Carlton said, his eyes twinkling with amusement.

"Oh, please," Jax said. "Now you're just trying to fit in with the rest of us."

"Seriously, golden boy," Pete agreed. "Give it up."

"Where are you from, Mia?" Leo asked.

"I've been living in New York City my whole adult life," I said.

"And you've finally decided to seek out greener pastures?" Jax asked.

"You can't do much better than Newberry," Carlton interjected. "It's got the right mix of bucolic and trendy."

Pete laughed. "I don't remember us singing that tune in high school. If I recall correctly, we were all going to make a break for it."

"Because we were young and stupid," Leo said. "It's a rite of passage to discover that you actually live in a desirable area."

"What do you do here?" I asked. Maybe one of these fine specimens could offer me a job.

"I'm a realtor," Jax said, "but I guess you've already got that part covered—unless you're renting with an eye to buy."

"I'm not renting," I said, keeping my answer deliberately vague. I didn't want to discuss my circumstances right now.

"I'm an accountant," Carlton said.

"And I'm a car salesman," Leo said. "The showroom is only twenty minutes from here if you're in the market."

Carlton slapped him on the back. "Gave me a great deal on my new Audi."

"Not now, but maybe down the road," I said. It would be good to know a car salesman.

"What can I get you to drink, Mia?" Pete asked. "Your first drink in Newberry is on the house."

"Thanks, how about a mojito?"

"Coming right up."

We chatted with the trio of suits for another few minutes and eventually drifted into our own clusters. The other men had started reminiscing about people only they knew, which was only really fun for them.

"I told you this place is lame," Patrick said, directing the remark to Scarlet.

"Madeline Albrecht would never approve of standing outside to drink in the middle of March."

"Who's that?" Scarlet asked.

"My mom. She's particular about the seasons and what's permissible during each one."

"Madeline Albrecht?" Patrick asked. "Wow. Your mom is a former Secretary of State?"

"No, she's the former secretary of the law firm of Struck & Schumer. Now she works part-time at the makeup counter at the mall. She likes the freebies and discounts."

"How does one go from defending the nation to defending her choice in eyeshadow?"

"Are you listening to me? She's Albrecht, not Albright. She's not at all bright, in fact, and Albrecht is the name of husband number three. Jurgen Albrecht. Dad died when I was twelve and Mom spent her time trying to replace him."

Scarlet's brow lifted. "Jurgen, huh?"

"He's a perfectly lovely man," I said. "Frankly, I don't know how she manages to keep attracting them."

"Probably because she knows the proper way to apply makeup," Patrick said pointedly.

"Wow," I said.

He sipped a flute of Aperol Spritz. "Scarlet can give you gardening lessons and I can offer you a makeup tutorial."

"Patrick, don't be rude," Scarlet admonished him. "Mia looks very pretty." She shifted her attention to me. "His tongue tends to loosen after a few drinks. You get used to it."

Patrick leaned over the counter and fluttered his eyes at the bartender. "How about now?" he asked, injecting a note of sweetness into his feathery-soft voice.

Pete wiped down the bar. "Fine, but stick to the classics. I don't want any complaints. It hurts my tips."

"You're the best." Patrick blew him a kiss and hustled over to the grand piano.

I cut a glance at Scarlet. "Is he really going to play?"

She folded her arms and leaned a hip against the counter. "Until we pry his moisturized hands away from the keys."

Patrick flexed his hands and then wiggled his fingers before tickling the ivories.

"Does he sing, too?" I whispered.

Scarlet smirked. "You'll see."

CHAPTER SIX

I WAS glad Stella warned me about the noisy pipes because I spent the first night in the house staring at the ceiling and praying the ornery cat didn't fall asleep on my face and suffocate me.

Background noise didn't tend to bother me. I'd spent my entire adult life in the midst of honking horns and the sounds of a bustling city. But the sounds of Red Clover were different. Dare I say it—even a tad eerie. It didn't help that I had a pounding headache thanks to the drinks and music at Jama. That being said, it had been fun listening to Patrick. He was a natural performer.

I huddled under the blankets and played Taylor Swift on my phone to keep the shivers at bay. I finally fell asleep and dreamed I was alone in Times Square. I stood in its center, surrounded by skyscrapers. A blast of air drew my attention to the top of the Marriott. There I saw a small black dot against the blue backdrop of the sky. The black spot moved and I realized with a start it was plummeting toward me. As it came closer, I was able to discern the white front and matching paws. Ophelia streaked toward me like a falling atom bomb and I did the only think I could think of—I held out my hands to catch her.

My eyes flew open and I immediately recognized the darkened master bedroom of Red Clover. Beads of sweat lined my brow and gathered under my boobs. From her position on my stomach, Ophelia lifted her head and regarded me curiously.

"What are you doing there?" I hissed. I was afraid to move and inspire an attack. Even in the darkness, I could see that she'd managed to track dirt onto the blanket. One night and I already needed to do laundry.

The cat dropped her head and closed her eyes. She felt like an anvil resting on my abdomen.

My head flopped against the pillow and I tried to get comfortable despite the immense pressure I felt on my stomach. Somehow, I managed to fall asleep and thankfully the remainder of my dreams was devoid of cats raining from the sky.

I woke up feeling groggy but reasonably rested. The cat was gone; the only evidence of her presence was the dirt she'd left behind. Better than a mouse head.

"Coffee," I said out loud. It occurred to me that I'd need to place an online order with a grocery store and quickly. Stella had been kind enough to stock the basics, knowing that the house had been unoccupied for months, but that only covered the basics. I was still in mourning; therefore, I was going to need chocolate and booze—and lots of them.

I wandered downstairs in a bit of a fog and rooted through the refrigerator and pantry to see what I could scrounge for breakfast. Scrambled eggs and a cup of tea would have to do.

Ophelia's bowls were empty, so I refilled one with water and the other with food, although I had no idea how many times a day a cat needed to eat. I'd have to consult the internet.

I went upstairs to wash my face, brush my teeth, and change into clothes that could withstand gardening. I didn't own a pair of sweatpants, so yoga pants would have to suffice.

I left the house in search of gardening tools. I decided to start with the small barn, fairly certain I'd seen a shovel in there yesterday. Maybe there'd be other items I could use as well. As I entered the barn to investigate my options, I saw an unexpected object in the corner—my transportation salvation.

"Score!"

I hurried over to examine the canary yellow motor scooter with a metal basket attached to the front.

"Is it a Vespa?" I wondered aloud. It was covered in cobwebs, so I didn't want to touch it with my bare hands. I noticed a pair of gardening gloves on a nearby box of crates and slipped those on before wiping away the silky threads.

Okay, it wasn't a Vespa, but it would do. A two-wheeled mode of transport made sense in a town like Newberry with its narrow roads and crowded main street. This must've been what Hazel used to get around before her eyesight began to fail.

"Mia?"

I spun around, startled. Scarlet stood in the open doorway of the barn, clutching a small potted plant.

"Sorry, I didn't mean to scare you."

"It's okay. I was just checking out my new set of wheels." I gestured to the yellow scooter. "I'll look like I'm riding on a ray of sunshine."

Scarlet smiled. "It's been years since I've seen it. Hazel used to ride it into town every day. You should have Buddy look at it and make sure it's roadworthy."

"Buddy?"

"He owns the auto body. Look up Buddy's Body Shop. Tell him you're Hazel's relative and he won't swindle you." The suggestion, of course, being that he would swindle me otherwise.

"Thanks for the tip."

"This is for you." Scarlet handed over the potted plant with a flourish. The green stems were short and stubby.

"Thanks, but you may have noticed I have an entire garden full of dead plants outside."

"And we'll tend to those soon enough." She motioned to the offering. "This is an aloe plant. It will be very hard for you to kill this one."

"Challenge accepted," I said. "Isn't aloe for sunburn?" I had memories of rubbing aloe vera all over my skin after ignoring my mother's warnings about the ability of the sun's rays to penetrate cloud cover. As usual, I'd tuned her out to my detriment.

"It also calms restless spirits," Scarlet said.

"It'd be more useful if it calmed restless leg syndrome." I wasn't the least bit worried about the ghost of Aunt Hazel coming to haunt me, mainly because I didn't believe in ghosts.

Scarlet ignored me. "You should talk to it. Give it a name."

"Give the plant a name?" I scoffed.

"A name," she repeated firmly. "It doesn't matter what. Prickly Pete will do."

"Wilson," I announced.

She shot me a quizzical look. "Ex-boyfriend?"

"No. Tom Hanks' friend in that movie where he's alone on the island."

Scarlet strangled a laugh. "The volleyball from Castaway?"

I pretended to pet the plant. "That's the one. I'd draw a face on it, but I don't think there's enough space."

She gave me an appraising look. "Interesting choice."

"Why?"

"Because the aloe plant is also used for protection and relief from loneliness." She cocked her head. "Are you sure you don't know anything about plants?"

"Not a thing."

"Hmm," Scarlet said, still regarding me closely. "You should take a moment to express your gratitude."

"I said thank you. What more do you want? A vial of blood?"

She laughed. "Not to me. To the plant."

My eyes widened at the aloe plant. "You want me to express gratitude to a plant?"

"Yes. Treat your plant the way you want to be treated," Scarlet said.

"I don't need people to thank me."

"Okay, so learn Wilson's needs and tend to them. That's the gist of it."

"Listen. I appreciate the gesture, but if you expect this plant to live, you need to keep it simple. Water once a day… That sort of thing. Once you add too many requirements, my brain switches off."

"I can see I have my work cut out for me when it comes to helping you with the garden," Scarlet said.

"I actually came in here to look for gardening tools."

Scarlet surveyed the barn. "You have everything you need in here, but I know there are more things in the shed."

"Good to know. Care to offer any hints? They all look the same to me."

Scarlet picked up a set of giant scissors. "These are hedge clippers."

"I knew a girl in high school who could've used a pair of

those to cut her hair. Her head was big enough to qualify as a float in the Macy's Thanksgiving Day parade." I set the plant in the basket of the scooter and took the clippers. "Care to show me how to use them?"

Scarlet's phone buzzed and she pulled it from her back pocket. "Hey, Todd. What's up?" She listened intently. "No problem. I'll be there in twenty minutes."

"Uh oh. Garden emergency?"

"A problem with the underground sprinkler at a client's house. I'm sorry but I need to go."

I stared at the clippers with mixed emotions. "That's okay. Maybe I'll wait on these. I don't need a catastrophic injury on day one."

"Did you sleep okay or was it hard to be in a strange place?"

"Oh, I've slept in my share of strange places," I said. "A beer-soaked floor, a bus station bench, the hammock of a hotel…"

Scarlet laughed. "Not me. I need a bed or I can't sleep a wink."

"Patrick did mention you like to have the feeling of control. You definitely don't get that trying to get your back comfortable on a bus station bench."

"Sounds like a good story," she said.

We vacated the barn and Scarlet guided me to the nearest section of the garden.

"My advice is to start here. It's full of weeds. If you focus on pulling those up, it'll be hard for you to accidentally destroy anything good."

I wagged a finger at her. "O ye of little faith."

She shaded her eyes from the stark sunlight. "I'd steer clear of the witch's garden until you know what you're doing. There are some delicate plants in there as well as poisonous ones. You don't want to end up in the hospital."

I offered a curious smile. "The witch's garden?"

"The area closest to the kitchen with the herbs," Scarlet said.

I glanced in that direction. "That's a cute name for it. Makes me feel like I live in a fairy tale cottage." I didn't realize there was actual terminology for different types of gardens. I learned something new every day.

"I need to get moving. Good luck and don't expect a miracle. This place is going to take time."

"No worries. I haven't expected a miracle since the time I stole Lindsey Hershberger's tooth from the lunch table and hid it under my pillow for the Tooth Fairy."

Scarlet's jaw unhinged. "You stole another child's tooth in order to get the money?"

I shrugged. "I was saving for a new doll. My mom said I had to pay for it myself or to wait for Christmas and I wasn't big on patience."

Scarlet resisted a smile. "They say it's a virtue."

"I've yet to be convinced."

She started toward the driveway. "Try not to hurt yourself. I'll see you later."

I heard the crunch of pebbles as she left and turned back to face my nemesis. I wasn't sure why I felt compelled to clean up this mess. It wasn't as though I was a neat freak or cared about nature other than the occasional selfie in Central Park when the lighting took ten years off my face. I wouldn't reap the benefit of any work for a full year. Still, I felt strangely obligated to restore this garden to its former glory.

I opened the YouTube app on my phone. If there was a video that explained how to load a dishwasher, then surely there was a video that explained how to reclaim your garden after an apocalypse or a similar event. I didn't need anything fancy, just the basics would be sufficient. After a solid ten minutes of searching without the desired results, I decided to start simple and eradicate the weeds as Scarlet suggested. With my luck, even if I managed to resurrect the garden, I'd end up creating some kind of mutant zombie plants that attacked people and took over the town.

The phone jingled with an incoming video call from my mother. Couldn't she text like a normal human? Reluctantly, I accepted the call and Madeline Albrecht's unlined face filled the screen. The woman looked straight out of a wax museum.

"Are you using a filter?" I asked.

"No, I had Botox a couple weeks ago so you're seeing my skin at its peak. Plus, I'm wearing a new foundation. Do you like it?" She stuck her nose closer to the camera. "It's called Bronze Goddess."

"I don't need to count your nose hairs, thanks."

"Where are you?" she asked, trying to peer around me like I was in 3D.

"In Aunt Hazel's garden, trying to spruce it up."

My mother tossed her head back and laughed uproariously.

"It's not *that* funny," I said.

"Do you even know the difference between a weed and a flower?"

"Of course. Weeds are ugly and flowers are pretty."

My mother's lips curved into a knowing smile. "Sure, honey. Go with that."

"I have a professional consultant, but I wanted to see what I could do on my own."

My mother leaned forward to scrutinize me. "Why would you do that?"

"Because I have time to kill—and weeds, apparently. If I have to stay here for a year, I might as well whip the place into shape so I can get top dollar for it."

"You never know, sweetheart. You might change your mind and decide to stay."

Now it was my turn to laugh. "This place isn't for me. It's pretty but full of nature." I missed the guy that loitered outside on Saturday night wearing mismatched clothes and singing charmingly off-key while strumming the lid of a pizza box like a ukulele.

"Have you met any nice young men yet?" my mother asked.

Naturally, my mind conjured up an image of a Hunka Hunka Burning Law, but I refused to share news of his existence with my mother.

"You have, haven't you?" The note of triumph in her voice was unmistakable.

"I haven't met anyone. I'm recovering from a painful breakup, remember? I proposed and was rewarded with public humiliation. The last thing I need is a new relationship."

"It's the *only* thing you need to forget that unremarkable man," she insisted. "Just be sure the new one is gainfully employed."

"Unlike me."

My mother smiled. "Well, that's only temporary, sweetie. Someone always gives you a chance, don't they? You have one of those faces."

I frowned and immediately regretted it. A woman shouldn't have more wrinkles than her mother. It was unnatural—like my mother's forehead.

"What's that supposed to mean?" I asked.

"Oh, honey. You know what I'm talking about. People are always willing to take a chance on an average-looking woman because they know you're willing to work harder to prove yourself. When someone's too attractive, they don't feel the need to make an effort because they assume their looks will carry them through. It's the same reason you never want to sleep with someone too good-looking, not that you have to worry about that."

I pressed my lips together to hold back the torrent of curse words congregating on my tongue.

"Listen, someone's at the door. Probably the deliveryman with my Sephora order. Gotta run!" She disappeared from the screen before I could say another word.

I lowered the phone, which was just as well because my arm was starting to tingle from overexertion. I should probably feel lucky she didn't call me ugly, at least not to my face. I had no misgivings about the way she likely talked about me to her husbands. Based on the look of surprise on Jurgen's face when I first met him, he'd expected a squat troll with an extra nipple and a hair growth issue.

A text from Tracy appeared, asking for an update on the house and the town. It was nice to have someone checking on me in an undemanding and non-critical way. I told her about the need to stay for a year and she sent a bug-eyed emoji in response. Her kids would probably love Red Clover. Maybe I'd invite them to visit once I was settled.

I used my phone to play background music, slipped on a pair of gardening gloves, and kneeled on a folded towel in front of the first row of plants. My upper body strength wasn't anything to brag about. Pulling up weeds was worse than trying to open a new jar of mayonnaise. Most of the time I failed to tear up the roots, which I knew meant the weeds would simply grow again in the same spot. At some point, Ophelia appeared next to the discarded debris. She meowed rather than hissed and I considered that progress.

"You could get yourself a pair of opposable thumbs and help me out," I said. "Lazy cat."

Ophelia settled on top of the pile of weeds like I'd

prepared a bed of roses for her. She regarded me with her intense green eyes.

"I don't know what I'm doing, so don't watch me for any tips." I continued struggling and swore when I developed a cramp in my hand. I removed a glove and massaged the injured base of my thumb. If this was the beginning of arthritis, I was moving straight back to the city. Newberry was aging me prematurely and I hadn't even been here a week.

I met Ophelia's inquisitive gaze. "What do you think I should do? You can't be too thrilled to have a new roommate. I know I wouldn't be." I once ended up sharing a sublet with a young woman from Russia who barely spoke English. It was hard enough to navigate a roommate situation at the best of times, but Svetlana and I couldn't understand each other. Even worse, she looked like a model, so the few times we went out together, I felt like an invisible woman. Men would push past me to reach her, as though I was an ottoman that blocked their way to the sleek leather sofa.

Ophelia said nothing in response. Instead, she dipped her head to lick her paw.

"Any suggestions for employment in this town? I get the sense that my prospects run the gamut from tattoo artist to thespian. I don't think I'm qualified for any of it. Is there a local newspaper?" Maybe they'd have an ad sales position for me there.

Ophelia closed her eyes, as though bored by my attempt at conversation.

"Did you like Hazel?"

At the mention of Hazel, Ophelia opened her eyes again.

"Aha. That got your attention." Although it freaked me out a little to know that the cat recognized names. What was next? The nuclear codes?

"I would like it if we could co-exist in peace. A detente, if you will. Like Gorbachev's Russia and Reagan's America."

Ophelia stood. It was hard to tell what she was doing given the size of her belly, but I soon realized she was stretching. She seemed calm and tolerant of me, so I took off my glove and attempted to pet her.

Bad idea.

She hissed and swatted at me, then bit my hand. Two sharp fangs went straight through the skin and I howled in pain. She picked up the glove in her teeth and ran, disappearing deeper into the garden.

"Ophelia! Come back with that." It took me longer than I cared to admit to rise to a standing position and I heard more than one popping sound.

I chased the cat through the garden, trampling the plants and weeds as I went. It didn't matter. I'd be yanking them up soon enough anyway, unless Scarlet returned to instruct me which ones to save.

For a cat the size of Garfield, Ophelia was surprisingly nimble and spry. It didn't help that I'd succumbed to the call of the carbs over the winter and packed on a few extra pounds. It seemed that the moment I passed forty, my body decided to retain water and fat as though I might have to make it through all my remaining winters without food. It was the hormonal equivalent of a life insurance underwriter calculating the number of years I likely had left and making the necessary adjustments in fleshy layers.

"Ophelia, where are you?" I tried to keep my voice light. Despite the throbbing pain in my hand, I refused to give the cat the satisfaction of knowing she'd hurt me. It reminded me of the time Lynette hired the spoiled daughter of a major client to work alongside me. I was meant to show her the ropes, but Cindy insisted on treating me like her assistant, despite my repeated attempts to steer her straight. I knew I had to grin and bear it or risk losing the client. Cindy knew that, too, and took full advantage. She wasn't as dumb as her stiletto-heeled snow boots suggested. Anyway, it wasn't easy, but I outlasted her. She quit by jetting off to Cannes for her annual month-long vacation and simply never reporting back to the office.

The cat managed to dart into a section of overgrown bushes. I pictured her rear-end sticking out like Winnie-the-Pooh when he overindulged in honey and couldn't quite make it all the way home.

"Ophelia, I'm not angry, just disappointed," I called, using an oft-used line by my mother.

I wasn't about to cut a path straight through the bushes, so I attempted to skirt the outer edge. Unfortunately, I wasn't watching the ground and managed to trip over a fallen log. I cried out as I fell and scraped my already injured hand on the earth. Who left a log in the middle of the garden? That was just asking for trouble.

It was only when I turned to glare at the offending tree limb that I realized I was wrong. It wasn't the limb of a tree at all.

It was the limb of a dead body.

CHAPTER SEVEN

"Well, isn't this a darn shame?" Chief Tuck Sherwood scratched his snow-white beard as he observed the woman's corpse. The chief of police stood about six feet tall with weathered skin and blue eyes that rivaled Paul Newman's. There was an unexpected sweetness to his manner given that he was the local chief of police.

"Do you know who she is?" I asked, unable to look at the dead body. The only dead bodies I'd seen were already in coffins in the middle of a funeral service. I wasn't accustomed to seeing them in the wild.

"Sure do," the chief said. "That's Gladys Spencer."

With her grey hair and sensible shoes, she looked like a Gladys.

"You don't know her?"

"No, I only arrived in town yesterday."

He glanced over his shoulder toward the house. "You bought this place or you're renting?"

"Neither. My father's aunt left it to me. She died a couple months ago and I'm her only living heir."

His thick white eyebrows seemed to rise like two puffy

clouds. "Hazel was your aunt?"

"My dad's aunt," I said. "I'm Amelia Thorne but everyone calls me Mia."

"You weren't here for the memorial service," he said. It almost sounded like an admonishment.

"No. I didn't know her."

He gave me a curious look. "Why not?"

"My family life is complicated."

Chief Sherwood appeared unmoved. "Family is important, Ms. Thorne. You're a grown woman. You couldn't reach out on your own?"

"My dad's been dead for a long time and my mom thought Hazel was cuckoo for Cocoa Puffs, so we never had any interaction with her."

"Gladys here was one of your aunt's best friends," he said. "Did you know that?"

"Obviously not. I just told you I didn't know her, so how would I know any of her friends?"

His expression sharpened. "That's a nasty mark on your hand. You should get that looked at."

I cradled my wounded hand. I'd been so shocked by the body that it seemed to numb the pain.

"Where'd you come from, Ms. Thorne?"

My mother's womb didn't seem like the answer he was looking for. "New York City."

"A lot of crime in the city. You're probably always looking over your shoulder, worrying about getting mugged—or worse."

I narrowed my eyes. "What's your point?"

"Maybe you saw someone trespassing on your new property and you got nervous. Reacted without thinking. Do you carry a weapon?"

"Does sarcasm count?"

The chief stared at me with a blank expression. "Maybe

you reacted by pushing her and she hit her head on one of those decorative rocks."

My eyes popped so hard, I worried they might freeze that way. "Are you accusing me of killing her?"

Chief Sherwood inclined his head. "Why don't you come down to the station and we can talk about it?"

I pointed at the dead woman. "Talk about this?" I heard my voice go up an octave and winced. I hated when my voice went high-pitched. I half expected dogs in the neighborhood to start howling in response.

"It's standard procedure," Chief Tuck said.

"Not for me. The closest I've gotten to a police station is…" I trailed off.

He narrowed his eyes. "Is when?"

"Nothing," I said quickly. If he didn't actually arrest me, he might not find out.

"I see."

"We can't leave now," I said. "What about the body?"

"Not to worry. I'll have it taken care of it."

"I don't have a car." A lame objection, but I didn't have a better one.

"I'll drive, Miss Thorne. The station's not very far."

"Okay then. I wouldn't want to inconvenience you, especially because you'll have to drive me home afterward."

He let me ride in the front seat, which was considerate and made me feel less like a murder suspect.

"There's an active theater community here," he said, pointing to the theater as we passed it. "Sunday matinees are the best time to go if you're looking to save money."

"Thanks for the tip."

"Do you kayak?"

I shot him a quizzical look. His disposition was awfully amiable for a man who thought I'd killed a helpless old woman.

"I've been once or twice on vacation. Not a lot of opportunity for it in the city."

"You'll appreciate it here," he said. "I like to fish from my kayak. I bring a nice picnic, toss out a small anchor, and relax for a few hours." He tapped his thumbs idly on the steering wheel. "The nice weather will be here soon enough."

We pulled into the station and he unlocked my door.

"You're not going to make a run for it, are you?" he asked. "My knees aren't what they used to be."

"I hear that." I popped open the door. "I'm not going to run because I'm innocent."

He said nothing as he left the vehicle and escorted me inside, directing me to a small interrogation room.

"I'll be with you in just a minute. Can I get you a drink? There's water or we have hot cocoa if you're in the mood for something sweeter."

I perked up at the mention of hot cocoa. "Do you have those little marshmallows?"

"I'm sure we can manage that."

"Thanks, Mr...I mean, Chief Sherwood."

"Everybody calls me Chief Tuck."

He sauntered out of the room and closed the door, leaving me alone at the table. I tried not to think about poor Gladys. How long had she been there? Days? Hours? She was wearing a coat, which suggested she hadn't been killed inside and then carried outside to dispose of the body.

As promised, Chief Tuck returned with a mug of hot cocoa covered in tiny marshmallows and placed it in front of me.

"You might want to wait a minute so you don't scald your tongue," he advised. "Apparently this isn't your first brush with the law."

My throat went dry. It was full cottonmouth, like that time I'd woken up in the morning after a night of tequila shots in Cabo. I'd been so drunk on the walk home from the beach bar that I'd stripped naked and jumped in the ocean before being carried back to my room by a beefy albeit well-mannered security guard. My friends had followed behind us with my clothes, snapping photos and cackling like two hyenas in stereo.

"I had a minor incident about ten years ago," I said. "Is that bad?"

Chief Tuck peered at me with those ice blue eyes. "You were arrested. You don't think that's bad?"

"I got probation," I said. "It couldn't have been that bad, right?"

"According to the report, you assaulted a man with an Indian cigar statue and called him a racist," Chief Tuck said.

"In my defense, I was very, very drunk." I paused.

"That explains the charge of drunk and disorderly."

"And I stand by my statement. Having that statue on display was insensitive to Native Americans. Anyway, I didn't exactly assault him with it. I pushed it over and it broke his toe."

The chief observed me in silence for a moment and I couldn't decide whether he thought I was innocent or an idiot. Maybe both.

"Murder is a big step from knocking over a racist statue," I said.

"I think you'll find most criminals start small and scale up over time," a voice said.

I glanced up to see an insanely attractive man in a suit. He swaggered into the room with the confidence of a former athlete who'd peaked in high school but didn't know it. It was actually kind of charming.

"Deputy coroner's at the scene, Chief," the former high school athlete said.

Chief Tuck nodded gruffly. "Good. We should know

cause of death in the next forty-eight hours." He motioned to me. "Detective Fairfax, this is Amelia Thorne, the new owner of Red Clover."

My radar pinged. "Fairfax? As in Dane Fairfax?"

He gave me a curious look. "I'm Derek, his younger brother."

I could see the resemblance. Slightly darker hair and an inch or so shorter but same build and Caribbean eyes. It seemed unfair to have such a high concentration of good genes in one family.

"You know Dane Fairfax?" Chief Tuck asked.

"I signed papers at his office yesterday."

"Have a seat, Fairfax," the chief said. "I was just discussing Ms. Thorne's criminal history with her."

"It's not really criminal history," I said. "Seriously. Who hasn't been drunk and disorderly at least once in their life?" I didn't like the way they were both looking at me. "I didn't kill anyone. I'm far too lazy for a felony. I don't even kill ants or spiders in the house, not because I respect their precious lives, but because it would involve getting off the sofa." I shook my head somberly. "I only get up if I really have to pee. And I mean really."

Chief Tuck exchanged glances with the detective. "I'm going to need a rundown of your schedule the past couple days. I'm also going to need you to stay put until we figure this out."

"That works for me," I said. "I can't go anywhere for a year."

Chief Tuck peered at me. "How's that?"

"I need to stay for a year in order to keep the house," I said. "I can't sell it until then."

"You want to sell?" Detective Fairfax asked, in a way that made me rethink that particular plan.

"That had been the plan, until I learned about the provision." My palms began to sweat at the thought of going to prison. "She could've been out there for days. I wasn't even in town until yesterday."

"Or she could've been killed last night or early this morning," Chief Tuck said. "We'll know more once the autopsy results are in. Anything else you care to share, Ms. Thorne?"

I slotted my fingers together on the table. "I don't know what else I can tell you. I've never seen the woman before. I literally tripped over her while chasing a cat. A cat, by the way, whose speed and stealth seem to defy physics."

"That's a nasty mark on your hand." Fairfax pointed at the red and swollen skin. "How'd you manage it?"

I held up the injured hand for closer inspection. "The aforementioned cat."

"We'll need confirmation that those marks are, in fact, from a cat," Fairfax said.

I gaped at him. "You think Agnes did this to me?"

"Gladys," Chief Tuck corrected me.

"Could be defensive wounds," Fairfax said.

"Yes, *my* defensive wounds," I countered.

"I recommend Dr. Farrell. She's smart and has a pleasant bedside manner," Chief Tuck said. "Her office is only two blocks from here." He glanced at Fairfax. "Why don't you call and see if you can get our friend in today? Sometimes it can be tough for a new patient to get an appointment."

"I'll have to check and see if she's on my insurance plan," I said. I now had COBRA thanks to the loss of my job and hadn't bothered to check the specifics.

Chief Tuck swatted the air. "It'll be fine. Go on ahead."

I looked warily from one to the other. "I can go?"

"Fairfax will accompany you. That way he can give you a lift home afterward." He turned slightly to address his underling. "You don't mind, do you?"

"No, sir. Of course not." Detective Fairfax gave me an expectant look. "You ready, Miss Thorne?"

I made sure to drain every last drop of hot cocoa from the mug.

"I am now."

"You dislike the doctor's office," I said. I wasn't sure where the statement came from. It seemed to bubble to the surface and slide off my tongue before I could stop it.

Detective Fairfax gave me an uneasy look. "What makes you say that?"

"I…I don't know. Something happened in your youth." Suddenly the peaking in high school description made sense. "You suffered an injury in high school. Football?"

"Soccer," he said. "Did Dane tell you that?"

"No," I said. "He didn't tell me anything about you."

A feeling of extreme discomfort overtook me and my head grew fuzzy. What was wrong with me?

"Amelia Thorne," the receptionist called, snapping me back to reality. "The doctor will see you now."

I rose to my feet and approached the door.

"Not you, Detective Fairfax," the receptionist said, smiling sweetly. "You know how privacy laws work. I'll be happy to keep you company while your friend is in the exam room."

From her predatory expression, I thought I might find her seated in his lap by the time I left the exam room.

I turned to wink at him. "You'll have to admire me in a paper gown some other time." I slipped through the door and was directed to a corner in the corridor with a scale.

"Let me just grab your height and weight," the nurse said.

I cringed. "Is that necessary?"

The nurse offered a sympathetic smile. "You can close your eyes if you like. I won't say the number out loud."

"Bless you," I said and slipped off my shoes. I wasn't willing to carry the extra pound or two onto the scale whether I heard the results or not.

Afterward the nurse pointed me to the adjacent exam room. I sat on the edge of the exam table, my legs dangling over the side, as the nurse checked my blood pressure.

"Do you normally have high blood pressure?"

"Not that I know of, but I've been under a lot of stress recently."

The nurse scribbled a few notes. "Dr. Farrell will be right in."

The nurse left and I stared at the wall, feeling out of sorts. A woman was murdered on my property. Aunt Hazel's friend. Yet I still had to remain in the house for a year or forfeit the inheritance. Maybe it wasn't worth it. Maybe I should leave town as soon as the police give their approval and move in with my mother and Jurgen.

My heart began to pound and I inhaled deeply in an effort to calm myself. The door swung open and the doctor entered the room. She was a petite woman with a head full of brown curly hair that reminded me of Andie MacDowell.

"Hi there. I'm Dr. Farrell. I understand you have an injury that needs assessment."

"I'm making friends with a resistant cat," I said, holding up my hand. "She's territorial."

The doctor inspected the skin of my hand. "When was your last tetanus shot?"

I swallowed hard. Needles still freaked me out thanks to a childhood bout of tonsillitis that ended in surgery.

"No idea," I croaked.

"You'll need one today then. Have you taken any painkillers?"

"I took ibuprofen and applied ice." I'd had the presence of mind to do that much after I went inside to call 911. "I think the police want confirmation that a human didn't do this to me."

Dr. Farrell eyed me curiously. "I see. Well, see these two puncture wounds?"

I nodded. It was hard to identify them due to the swelling, but I saw them.

"This clearly indicates a cat bite."

I shot a triumphant look at the wall, knowing the detective was seated somewhere on the other side of it.

"I'm also going to write you a prescription for amoxicillin. You're not allergic to penicillin, are you?"

I shook my head.

"Which pharmacy do you use?"

"I only moved here yesterday. I'll use whichever one you recommend."

Great. A tetanus shot, pills, and a dead body. Welcome to the neighborhood.

"I can't die from a cat bite, can I?" I asked. My hypochondriac tendencies started to kick in.

"It's possible but unlikely. If the cat has an infection, it can make its way into your bloodstream, but those cases are rare. That's why I'm giving you the shot as well as the prescription, to be on the safe side."

I tried to steady my breathing. No one knew me here. I was going to drop dead of an infection in the middle of the night and no one would know for days. Maybe even weeks. Ophelia would dine on the meat of my bones for months, which was probably her plan all along. Evil cat.

I left the exam room after the nurse administered the tetanus shot. Detective Fairfax was chatting with an attractive woman in the waiting area, but he stopped talking when he saw me.

"You okay?" he asked. To his credit, he actually seemed concerned.

"It's definitely a cat bite. I authorized the doctor to share the report with your office."

He nodded and stood, his keys already in his hand. "How about I drive you home now?"

"Mind if we stop at the pharmacy first?"

"No problem." He held the door open for me.

"This really hasn't been my day," I said.

His handsome face darkened. "I think Gladys Spencer might feel the same—if she could feel anything at all."

CHAPTER EIGHT

I WAS grateful when Scarlet and Patrick stopped by later. They'd heard about Gladys and wanted to check on me.

"To add insult to injury, they think I killed her," I said.

Patrick inclined his head. "Okay, so did they actually arrest you and, if so, who placed the handcuffs on you and how rough were they? I need a visual."

"They didn't arrest me, but Chief Tuck questioned me and Detective Fairfax drove me to the doctor's so I could get treatment for this." I held up my bandaged hand.

Scarlet winced. "Ophelia?"

I nodded. "So much for the cat recognizing me as Aunt Hazel's blood relative. The police thought my injury was from Gladys fighting me off."

"Good thing I brought you something that might help you bond with Ophelia." She handed me a gold-colored sachet.

"Catnip?" I asked.

She nodded. "Sprinkle these dried leaves in her favorite spots."

I sniffed the sachet. It smelled somewhat like tea leaves.

"And this will make her like me?" I asked, unconvinced.

"Not a guarantee, but it can't hurt," she said.

"Did Chief Tuck say it's definitely murder?" Patrick asked.

"No, but it's a suspicious, unattended death," I said, repeating a phrase I'd heard in the police station. "The autopsy results will hopefully shed more light on it."

"I can't believe you found her in your garden," Scarlet said. "That's so scary."

"I can't believe they think I killed her," I shot back. "The police cordoned off half the garden so at least I have an excuse to avoid it."

"Come to my house," Scarlet urged. "Take a break from this house."

Patrick lit up. "Yes, let's do that. I have an idea that might help. We're going to help solve the case."

I frowned. "'We' as in 'not the police?'"

"Definitely not. We have something they don't."

"Good hair?"

"Well, naturally, although Derek Fairfax is a close second. But I can offer something even better." He clasped his hands and flexed them forward. "I'm a ghost whisperer."

"A ghost whisperer," I repeated.

"Yes, and we're going to hold a seance. That way we can get answers directly from the source."

I suppressed a laugh. "Your plan is to summon the ghost of Gladys during a seance and have her tell us who killed her?"

"Pretty much," Patrick said.

"Like the movie *Ghost*," I said. I quickly became distracted by the awesomeness that was Patrick Swayze. *Ghost*, *Dirty Dancing*, the *North and South* miniseries...My eyebrows shot up. "While you're working your spirit mojo, any chance you can contact Patrick Swayze, too?"

"Don't I wish?" the non-Swayze Patrick said. "Believe me, I've tried."

I didn't object to the idea, as crazy as it sounded. Distancing myself from the scene of the crime appealed to me more than I cared to admit.

"I'll drive," Scarlet said.

Patrick smirked. "Of course you will."

We piled into Scarlet's car and drove along River Road to her house. I watched the scenery roll from the back seat. Even through a haze of painkillers and fear, I recognized the beauty of Newberry.

Scarlet's home was no less beautiful. Surrounded by lush gardens, the multi-story house sported three terraces to maximize the views and solar panels affixed to the roof. Unlike the riverfront position that Patrick and I had, Scarlet's house was set alongside a generous creek with a towpath that ran between the house and the water. There was also an enormous greenhouse in the yard bursting with life.

"How old is this place?" I asked, gazing at the dark red wooden building with its grey shutters.

"It's the old grist mill," Scarlet said. "It dates back to 1790 and was converted to a house in 1870 and then updated about twenty-five years ago."

"It's so cool," I said.

"I grew up in an old house in Lancaster County and I wanted something that reminds me of home," she said.

"Lancaster County? Isn't that Amish country?"

Scarlet smiled. "I'm clearly not Amish. My mom's parents came from China and my dad's side came from England. I learned all about flowers from my mother and grandmother."

"Tell her your Chinese name," Patrick prodded.

Scarlet's cheeks colored. "Fang. It means fragrant plants or agreeable."

"Fang," I repeated.

"Only my grandmother called me that." She paused. "But she's dead now."

"I'm sorry." My own grandparents were long gone and I'd barely known them, so it was hard to muster the same emotions Scarlet plainly felt for her grandmother.

"Scarlet watched this house like a hawk for years," Patrick said, "waiting for it to come on the market."

"I just hoped that the owners decided to sell at the same time I had enough money to buy it." She smiled as she surveyed the property. "Thankfully, it all worked out."

"I can see why you want to get your hands on Aunt Hazel's garden. You obviously have a knack."

Scarlet unlocked the front door. "Thank you. It's my passion."

She pushed open the door and I stepped into an open-plan living space with a dramatic twenty-foot stone fireplace. French doors along the back wall led to the middle-covered terrace.

I whistled. "Wow. This is stunning." Despite the high ceilings, the room maintained a cozy atmosphere.

Scarlet fingered the black stone on her necklace. "It took a lot of work to get it exactly the way I wanted, but I think I managed."

"We can admire your handiwork later," Patrick said. "We have a seance to perform."

"You'll need something from my stash," Scarlet said.

I assumed she meant drugs because that was the only way I imagined I'd see a ghost during a seance.

Scarlet guided us through the chef-style kitchen to a sun-drenched room. I immediately threw up my hands to cover my eyes, prompting laughter from Patrick. I peeked at him between my fingers to see he was now sporting sunglasses.

"You've obviously been in this room before," I said. I fished my sunglasses from my purse and slid them on to avoid the blinding flashes of light and color. A display of colorful crystals caught the natural light. I also spotted incense, lotions, and ointments. The only thing missing was a cauldron.

"Oh, this reminds me…" Scarlet contemplated a row of shiny stones. "You should take six quartz crystals to place around the garden."

"This is part of your landscape design?"

She turned to face me. "No, it will cleanse the energy from the space. Between Hazel's death and the murder of Gladys, that garden has to be awash with bad juju."

I pondered the selection of crystals. "You choose. I have no idea."

"Why don't you see if any speak to you?" Scarlet urged.

I laughed. "If any speak to me, then you'd better call a psychiatrist and have her order me a pill cocktail."

Scarlet didn't push the issue. Instead, she carefully chose six crystals, placing them into a purple pouch made of crushed velvet.

"Once the police have cleared the area, I'll show you where to put them," she said.

"How did you decide which ones to choose?" I asked, curious.

Scarlet smiled, appearing pleased by my interest. "A combination of knowing what the goal is and exploring the vibes for the most suitable ones."

Crystals. Vibes. Seances. I was completely out of my depth here. *Hippies*, my mother would say in her scathing voice.

While Patrick selected a crystal for the seance, I poked my head into the adjoining room. The shelves were lined with dark-colored glass bottles arranged in size order.

"This is where I keep my essential oils," Scarlet said.

"You make all those?" I asked.

Scarlet smiled proudly. "I do."

"Most women have a crafts room, not a craft room."

Scarlet turned one of the bottles so that the label faced front. "I'm not most women and neither are you."

"And here I thought your talents were limited to a green thumb."

"It's a calling," Scarlet said.

We returned to the sunlit room where Patrick had opted for a pale pink crystal. "I think this one is most likely to attract her spirit."

"I wish we could wait until Wednesday," Scarlet said.

Patrick gave her a pointed look. "What if they decide to arrest Mia tomorrow? Do you want that on your conscience? I think not."

"No, but Wednesday is the best day for spells that involve communication. It might be our best chance to speak to Gladys."

Patrick heaved a dramatic sigh. "Scarlet is somewhat of a stickler when it comes to timing."

"If you plant a flower at the wrong time, it won't flourish. You need to choose the best possible time to increase your chance of success."

"And hump day is best for communing with the spirits?" I queried.

She ticked off the options on her fingers. "Monday is for healing. Tuesday is for protection, Wednesday is best for communication or travel. Thursday is prosperity. Friday is for personal growth. You get the idea."

I clucked my tongue. "I hope you don't cut yourself on a Tuesday because then you need to wait almost a full week until you can heal yourself. You might be dead by then."

"But at least you'll have someone to talk to on Wednesday," Patrick interjected, grinning.

Scarlet glowered at us. "Make fun all you want."

"Oh, I do," Patrick said.

"The moon phases are important to consider, too," Scarlet said to me. "If you want to attract something to you, you want the waxing moon. If you want extra power, then wait until the full moon."

"Is there a special calendar for that?" I asked.

"I have an app on my phone," Scarlet said. "I can show you and then you can download the same one."

I smiled. "I'm good, thanks." I was starting to understand my mother's attitude toward Aunt Hazel. I mean, I liked Patrick and Scarlet, but they seemed to be living in an alternate reality from me.

We walked back through the house and Scarlet stopped in the kitchen to offer us food and drink. I accepted an unsweetened iced tea even though I would've preferred two teaspoons of sugar.

"I'm worried the cops aren't going to consider anyone else if they're focused on me," I said.

Patrick sipped his iced tea. "Then I guess that only leaves one option."

"Change my name to Amaya St. John and move to the Seychelles?"

He looked at me with amused interest. "No, but I like your style. My getaway plan is to change my name to Roderick Templeton and move to Mykonos."

I smiled. "Roderick Templeton, huh? Like a soap opera star. I can see that."

"No offense, but I don't see you as an Amaya St. John. Where'd you come up with that name?"

"I don't know. It was my fake dating name when I was younger."

Patrick beamed. "Same."

I gulped down the iced tea so fast that I barely tasted it. "I can't go to prison. I have to pee too frequently to wear a one-piece jumpsuit."

Patrick splayed a hand against his chest. "Personally, I never understood the onesie craze and I'm glad it's behind us now."

I hung my head. "What will I do?"

Scarlet refilled my glass. "It's going to work out. The real killer will be found and get you off the hook."

"How can you be so sure it isn't me?" I asked. "You only just met me."

"I have a sixth sense," Patrick said. "The spirits are telling me you're innocent…" He lowered his gaze. "And that you need to shave your legs."

I glared at him. "It's March. Of course I need to shave my legs."

"Ah. That might explain why your boyfriend decided to make a staffing change."

"If Andrew broke up with me over hairy legs, then good riddance to him." Good riddance to him anyway. I wouldn't want him back now, even if he showed up with a three-carat diamond and a lifetime supply of Reese's peanut butter cups.

We finished our drinks and continued through the house to a wooden staircase.

"There are two staircases on either side of the house," Scarlet said.

We arrived at a room decorated with deep autumnal colors. There was an oversized chaise lounge in a deep cranberry color, a sumptuous settee, an antique highboy dresser, a table with four upholstered oval-back chairs, a console table, and an array of abstract artwork on the walls. The heavy golden drapes added another touch of glamour.

"This is such a cool space," I said.

"I like to read in here," Scarlet said.

Patrick snatched a glamorous crystal perfume bottle off

the console table and squeezed the atomizer, releasing an intense fragrance. Cedarwood. Jasmine. Rose. Each scent seemed stronger than the next.

Scarlet groaned. "Did you eat broccoli again?"

He scowled at her. "No, this is for the spirit."

"Perfume attracts spirits?" I queried. The scent was certainly powerful enough to draw attention.

He spritzed the air around my head. "No, I've found that ghosts have odors and I want to preemptively diffuse Gladys's old lady smell. I have an extremely sensitive gag reflex."

I gave him a sympathetic look. "That's unfortunate." I patted my purse. "Let me know if you need reinforcements. I keep a stash with me at all times thanks to my mother's free samples."

Patrick smiled. "I knew I liked you." He turned and scrutinized the table. "This won't do."

I shot him a quizzical look. "It's a table. What could possibly be wrong with it?"

"It's all wrong for this."

"Then maybe we should conduct the seance at your house," Scarlet said archly.

Patrick whirled around and began rooting through the drawers of the highboy dresser. He pulled out a gold cloth and covered the table with it. "That's better."

I frowned at him. "How is that better?"

"The grain of the wood was too distracting. It reminded me too much of Clint Eastwood's wrinkled face. I didn't want to accidentally channel him."

"That might be difficult since he's still alive," Scarlet said.

Patrick smoothed the creases from the cloth and placed a chunky white candle in the center, as well as the pale pink crystal.

"What else do you need?" I asked. "A Ouija board?"

He gave me a droll look. "Hardy har. I can hardly breathe from the force of my laughter." He glanced at my clothes. "I'm not sure about your outfit."

I barked a short laugh. "Is it a black tie event?"

"I just think the spirits appreciate it when we dress up for the occasion," he said.

"Somehow I don't think it's the spirits who like when you dress up," I said.

"Scarlet, do you have something she can borrow?" Patrick asked.

"She's a little taller than me, but I'm sure I can find something." She headed into the hallway and I trailed behind her.

"Is this really necessary?" I asked.

"Probably not, but he enjoys elevating the dramatic elements and I don't have the heart to stop him." She crossed the threshold of the master bedroom and went straight to a walk-in closet.

I marveled at the interior space. The organized closet looked straight out of an 'After' segment on HGTV. The clothing was organized by color and fabric and there were shelves for accessories and shoes. Basically, there was a place for everything and everything in its place.

"This is amazing," I said. "Did you do this yourself?" I'd never seen a closet this big and tidy except on television or in magazines.

"I had help," she said. "It's important to me to stay organized. It helps the flow of energy. Clutter in this space begets clutter in this space." She tapped the side of her head.

Hmm. That explained a lot about me.

"I think the right hat will be enough to placate him," Scarlet continued.

"Like what? A pointy witch hat?"

Scarlet stood on a step stool and retrieved a transparent container from a shelf. "No, just something that makes a statement." She opened the lid and produced an oversized black hat adorned with elegant black feathers.

"That certainly does make a statement," I said. I placed the hat on my head. "What do you think? Ghosts galore?"

"It suits you."

Something about her smile gave me pause. "What is it?" I asked.

"The hat belonged to Hazel. She left it here after a party one year but wouldn't let me return it. She felt that the hat wanted to stay."

That was a clever way of getting rid of items you didn't want. If only it worked with body fat. *I'd love to take these love handles home with me, but they've told me they really want to stay here in the Italian restaurant.*

"I don't mind wearing it for the seance, but if Aunt Hazel felt that the hat belongs here, remind me not to leave with it."

Scarlet looked at me for an extended moment. "We'll see." She turned and pulled a hanger off the rod. "This is my seance outfit." The red beaded dress would have been at home at a party on the Upper East Side.

"It's gorgeous," I said.

"Are you sure you don't want to change clothes? I have plenty of dresses. They're sort of an addiction."

"They're very pretty, but one of your dresses would be a tube top on me."

"Fair enough." She stripped down to her undergarments without hesitation.

"Oh, we're doing this right now? Okay." I spun around to avoid ogling her perfect body. I didn't need a glimpse of Scarlet to remind me of my lumps and bumps. Clearly she had age and a favorable gene pool on her side. I had wacky hormones and a deep, enduring love of carbs on mine.

We returned to the glamour room and my eyes widened at the sight of Patrick.

"What?" he asked with an air of indignation.

"You've somehow morphed into Marlena Dietrich in a matter of minutes," I said.

Patrick wore a stark white turban cinched together by a sparkling red stone. His makeup was equally dramatic, with thick black eyeliner and mascara that made it look like he had two spiders stuck to his eyelids.

"The spirits demand respect and I show them respect by dressing appropriately," he huffed, jerking the drapes closed.

I didn't bother to ask where he'd been hiding his turban.

He motioned for us to sit. Then he lit the candle and placed his phone on the table.

"Shouldn't we put our phones away?" I asked.

"Oh, the ringer is off," Patrick said. "This is for mood music." He tapped the screen and music began to play softly in the background.

Scarlet rolled her eyes. "I thought we talked about Enya."

"We talked about it and agreed to disagree," Patrick said.

"Seems like you've really got a solid system in place," I said, impressed.

"You say that as though you doubt my expertise," Patrick said.

Scarlet leaned over. "Please don't doubt his expertise or we'll have to hear about it for the next twenty minutes."

"I'm simply admiring your process," I said.

Patrick held out his hands for Scarlet and I to take one. When I clasped his hand, he frowned at me. "If you need lotion, I can recommend an excellent brand that isn't too expensive."

"What makes you think I need lotion?"

"Because I feel like I've grabbed a snake in the desert."

"I feel slimy?"

"No, that's a common misconception," he said. "Snakeskin is actually dry."

"We can swap places," Scarlet offered. "You can hold the bandaged hand."

Patrick scrunched his nose. "No thanks."

He closed his eyes and began to hum. I looked at Scarlet, silently asking if we needed to hum too. She nodded, so I closed my eyes and joined the sound. It was only after a full minute that I realized my hum had morphed into the theme song from *Friends*—and that I was the only one still humming.

I peeked one eye open to find Patrick and Scarlet staring at me in silence. Well, Scarlet was staring. Patrick was glaring.

"Sorry, I don't hum a lot," I said. It wasn't the first time I'd turned a meditative hum into a theme song either. There was a yoga teacher in New York that I was certain had blackballed me from classes after a similar incident.

"We gather together to call forth the spirit of Gladys Spencer," Patrick said in an ominous tone.

A shiver traveled down my spine. What if it worked? What if a ghost appeared and identified her killer? How would we use that as evidence to convince the police and, even more crucially, how would I not pee my pants at the sight of a ghost?

I'd never seen a ghost—I didn't even believe in them—yet here I sat in a feathered hat listening to Patrick's dulcet tones, waiting for Gladys Spencer to shimmer into view and tell us what happened. One flash mob proposal and poor taste in men and this was my life now.

"Commune with us, sweet Gladys. We bring you gifts that you may bring with you into the afterlife."

I arched an eyebrow at the mention of gifts. It didn't seem smart to lure a ghost here under false pretenses. What if spectral Gladys got angry when she discovered it was a ruse?

On the other hand, we were trying to solve her murder. Arguably that was a gift.

"We await your presence," Patrick continued.

"Maybe you should've chosen a blue crystal," I whispered.

Patrick shushed me and called again for Gladys's spirit to join us.

A silhouette appeared behind Scarlet and the air escaped from my lungs. I opened my mouth to scream but no sound came out.

"I think we should call it," Scarlet said glumly. "Maybe try again on Wednesday."

I couldn't find my voice to tell her that someone was in the room with us.

"I have plans on Wednesday," Patrick whispered.

I released my hand to point at the silhouette just as it dissipated. I gripped the edge of the table instead.

"Mia, are you okay?" Scarlet asked.

"Yes, fine." I shook off my discomfort. Whatever I thought I'd seen was gone now.

"I'm sorry it didn't work," Scarlet said. "Maybe she's not ready to come to us."

Patrick ripped the turban off his head and flung it onto the table. "Or maybe I suck."

"You don't suck," I said quickly.

If that silhouette had belonged to Gladys, then Patrick had done his part. I pinched the bridge of my nose. What was I thinking? Of course that wasn't an old lady's ghost. It was a trick of the light. An illusion. Andrew always accused me of being a highly suggestible person. It was the reason he refused to let me accompany him to Las Vegas for a work trip a few months ago. He said he didn't want to have to hide my cash and credit cards to keep me from losing all my money. Now that I thought about it, though, I realized that he'd probably taken his new girlfriend to Vegas instead and that had been the real reason. He'd cheated on me and used an unfair criticism of me to cover his tracks. Wow. This seance didn't suck. *Andrew* sucked.

"There are other things we can try," Scarlet said in a cheerful tone.

"That's right," I said. "There's more than one way to skin a cat." I immediately cringed at my poor choice of words. Good thing Ophelia wasn't within earshot or I'd probably find cat vomit on my pillow tonight.

"For what it's worth," Scarlet said, "I don't need a ghost to tell me you didn't kill anyone."

"Thanks, Scarlet. I appreciate that."

Scarlet and I looked at Patrick expectantly.

"What?" he said. "Obviously I don't think she's guilty, but it would be nice to have Gladys confirm it."

"Gee, thanks for the vote of confidence," I said.

"I can drive you home," Scarlet said, "unless you'd rather stay here until the police figure things out. There's plenty of room."

"I appreciate the offer, but who knows how long that might take?" I also worried that living elsewhere would trigger the provision that prevented me from owning the house.

It was only after Scarlet dropped me off at Red Clover that I realized I was still wearing the black plumed hat. I smiled to myself as I removed the hat and placed it on a side table. It seemed that the hat wanted to return home after all.

CHAPTER NINE

I MUST'VE GOTTEN up at least five times in the night and I couldn't blame my bladder or hot flashes. Every sound seemed to bring the threat of a ghost or murder. Ophelia wisely didn't make an appearance. She probably realized that biting me was the wrong move. I'd also left catnip on the window seat so she might've spent the night downstairs in a dopey fog.

The sound of the doorbell jolted me upright in bed. I was surprised when I glanced at my phone and noticed it was eight o'clock. Still, who would turn up unannounced at this hour?

I grabbed a robe off the hook on the closet door and cinched it around me as I made my way downstairs. I'd worn plaid pajama pants so my hairy legs were concealed from view. There was nothing I could do about my tangled mess of hair on my head, though. If I frightened away the visitor, then they deserved it for showing up this early.

Ophelia stood sentry at the front door. She meowed at me as I brushed past her and opened it.

"Detective Fairfax. A little early, isn't it?"

His gaze flicked over my appearance. "Your property is a crime scene. There's no such thing as too early."

"Would you like to come in? I haven't made coffee yet, but I'm about to."

"Don't mind if I do." He swaggered into the house and I could see his eyes darting left to right—checking for clues, I guess. Well, I had nothing to hide, except my legs.

He followed me into the kitchen where I retrieved the ground coffee from the cabinet.

"How's your hand?" he asked.

"Sore, but better, thanks."

"I can make the coffee, if that would be easier."

I cut a glance over my shoulder. Was this a gentlemanly offer or a sneaky detective one? I couldn't decide. I stepped away from the coffee machine.

I watched him carefully measure out the scoops and tip them into the filter.

"Thought you'd want to know the preliminary results of the autopsy."

"Already?" I asked.

His focus shifted to me. "It's not the official report, just the preliminary findings. It isn't every day we get a case like this. It's a priority."

"Makes sense."

He turned on the coffee machine and opened the cupboard above it. "Where are your mugs?"

I pointed to the cupboard next to the refrigerator.

"Why do you keep them over there if the coffee machine is here?"

"That's where Aunt Hazel kept them, apparently. I haven't rearranged anything yet."

He crossed the kitchen and retrieved two mugs. I watched with amusement as he deliberated over the designs before choosing an owl mug and a cat mug.

"They put the time of death between six and eight on Thursday evening."

"Thursday evening? I wasn't even in town yet. Now you have to rule me out."

"Can you prove that?"

"Of course. I took a train to Princeton and then a car to Newberry on Friday. I met Stella and she drove me to the house. Then I signed papers at your brother's office."

"Yes, I spoke to my brother about it," he said in a tone I couldn't quite identify.

"And he confirmed my story, right?"

"He did." Detective Fairfax filled both mugs and grinned as he handed me the cat mug. "Figured you'd want this one."

"Funny."

We leaned against the counter, sipping coffee and eyeing each other. Was there chemistry between us or was it my imagination? Was it possible to have chemistry with a certain segment of DNA? That would explain the attraction to the Fairfax brothers. Then again, it could be the fact that they were both scorching hot.

"Do you have your train ticket with the date?"

"I'm sure I do. I'm not good at throwing things away." My purse was filled with relics of my past, including a tin of mints with only one mint left that I saved for bad breath emergencies, receipts from every store where I'd made purchases over the past three months, sample perfumes, a comb, three pens—one which ran out of ink last year, and a handful of coins. I had no doubt the ticket stub would be among the contents.

"I'll wait if you want to find it now."

I set down the mug and went to search my purse on the opposite counter. I found the stub of the train ticket wedged in one of the tiny pockets that seemed to serve no purpose whatsoever.

I took a photo of the stub with my phone before handing it over.

He chuckled. "Don't you trust me?"

"I don't think you're trying to frame me, but if your office is anything like mine, it might disappear into a black hole never to be seen again."

He swilled another mouthful of coffee. "My office is nothing like yours."

"Good to know." I popped off the lid to the amoxycillin and swallowed the pills with coffee.

"The victim died of severe injury to her head. We think someone hit her in the side of the head with an object of some kind."

"An object doesn't really narrow it down. I mean, a pencil is an object."

He pressed his lips together. "I can confirm it wasn't a pencil. We're searching the property for a shovel or a hoe—something that might've been used as a weapon. I have a warrant to check the outbuildings and we're combing the gardens, too. It's a jungle, though. Hard to see anything on the ground."

"You'll have to ask Stella whether the outbuildings have been locked up since Aunt Hazel's death. They were open when I got here, and friends of hers had been coming and going to feed the cat."

"Friends like Gladys."

I remembered Stella's surprise at the empty bowls upon my arrival. "I bet Gladys was on her way to feed Ophelia when she was killed. That's why she was in the garden."

Detective Fairfax continued to drink his coffee, but I could tell he was listening intently. "There's more."

"Okay."

"You need to take your cat to a vet."

I glanced at the empty doorway as though Ophelia might appear. "Why?"

"Because Gladys's head wound was infected with a bacteria carried by cats called *Pasteurella multocida*."

"Oh." An uneasy feeling crept over me. "Is it possible that Ophelia attacked her and caused Gladys to fall and hit her head?"

"It's possible, but we haven't found any evidence on the ground to explain the injury. There were rocks nearby but none with blood."

"Then what? You think Ophelia scratched her after she fell?" I wouldn't put it past her.

"Just get the cat checked out." He inclined his head. "Might want to check that hand of yours for an infection, too."

I'd been taking painkillers around the clock in addition to the amoxycillin, so I hadn't given myself time to feel anything. I unwrapped the bandage to inspect the wound. It seemed red and swollen, but it was hard to know whether that was from an infection or the bite itself.

"I'm already taking medicine for it, so I don't think there's anything else to do." I plucked a banana from the fruit bowl and peeled it. I needed food in my stomach to absorb all these pills. "Any other theories?"

"A few. She didn't weigh much. The killer might have hit her somewhere else and carried her to a more overgrown part of the garden and left her there, hoping it would take longer to find the body."

"Yeah, I'm not skilled in the art of murder, but if I had done it, I certainly wouldn't leave her on my own property. I would've driven her somewhere."

He snorted. "On your scooter? I don't think she would've fit in the wicker basket."

I glowered at him. "I'll have you know that basket is metal, not wicker."

He chuckled. "You're not helping your case. You don't have a vehicle capable of transporting a dead body. Your only option would've been to drag her into the bushes."

"Good thing we've already ruled me out then, isn't it?" I shoved the banana into my mouth and practically swallowed it whole.

Detective Fairfax raised his eyebrows. "That was almost pornographic."

My cheeks burned. "I have an appetite."

"Not helping." He polished off the rest of the coffee and rinsed his mug in the sink.

"Why are you here instead of Chief Tuck? I would think the chief of police would want to handle a priority case."

Detective Fairfax raked a hand through his hair. "Chief Tuck is a good cop, but everybody knows he'd prefer to be retired."

"Then why isn't he?" I asked.

The detective shrugged. "Because he's stubborn, which is part of what makes him a good cop."

"Well, thanks for the update."

"Thanks for the ticket stub." He patted his pocket. "Maybe after this is all over, you and I can go out for a drink. I know all the best watering holes in town."

"Your brother's the one who suggested Jama to me. He said you like it there."

He brightened. "I do. Dane wouldn't be able to recommend anywhere. It would require him to unchain himself from his desk."

"He's a workaholic, huh?"

"He was the same way in school. He'd study in the library until they kicked him out."

"I love the library," I said, which reminded me I needed to apply for a local library card.

"I guess you two have that in common." He paused. "He wanted to ask you out, you know. Chickened out." Detective Fairfax broke into a broad grin. "His loss."

I stared at him for a long moment, a realization stirring. "Is that why you broached the topic of asking me out? To beat him to the punch?" Claim his territory?

He winked and sauntered toward the doorway. "A little sibling rivalry is good for the soul."

No wonder he'd been willing to overlook my current state. I mean, face it. I was a complete mess. Banana or no banana, no man in his right mind would look at me now and think, *yes. I want to canoodle with that one*. Still, the detective was punching above my usual weight. So was Dane for that matter. Why was I attractive to men in Newberry who wouldn't have looked at me twice in the city? Did I inadvertently bathe in some sort of country catnip for men? My mind lingered on Dane Fairfax a little longer than necessary. I wish he had asked me out, but it sounded like he was married to his career. It wouldn't be the first time I'd been drawn to a man who was more interested in his job than he was in me.

My gaze fell upon my injured hand and I sighed. The Fairfax brothers were not my priority. The possibly diseased cat, on the other hand, was. I hurried upstairs to shower and change before I texted Stella for the name of the vet. Hopefully I could get an appointment today. The more information we gathered, the sooner the police could get answers—and the sooner I could sleep through the night.

CHAPTER TEN

Getting Ophelia to the vet took more strategy and gymnastics than I'd anticipated. I felt like I was preparing for battle. My limited experience with animals was catching up with me. Apparently cats didn't just come when you called them and they certainly didn't voluntarily walk into a crate in order to go to the vet.

Suddenly I remembered the catnip from Scarlet. I wasn't really sure how catnip worked, only that it was supposed to make Ophelia like me more—the way my bitchy college roommate Ava liked me more whenever she was drunk. That being said, the only diseases I'd worried about contracting from Ava had been STIs from sharing a bathroom, no matter how impossible it was according to the campus nurse.

I dangled a sachet in front of the open crate door. "Here, kitty. Come get your drugs."

Ophelia licked her paws and tossed me a lazy look. Nope. She wasn't buying what I was selling.

I tossed the catnip into the crate to see if that enticed her. When that failed, I resorted to the internet for answers. According to the many, many videos on YouTube, cats were afraid of cucumbers, although I didn't see how that would help me. I'd have to get the cat close enough to the crate that she'd leap backward into it to get away from the cucumber and I didn't think I could orchestrate that exact outcome.

A quick glance at the phone told me time was running out. I didn't want to risk being late and miss the appointment.

"Beggars can't be choosers," I said.

Grabbing the blanket from the back of the couch, I pounced on the cat like I was a fireman putting out flames. I wrapped it firmly around her whole body to prevent her claws and teeth from doing further damage.

I lifted the cat burrito and lugged it to the crate, stuffing the bundle inside and locking the door. Ophelia quickly shook off the blanket and glared at me resentfully.

"It's for your own good," I said.

The cat seemed unconvinced, yowling in protest.

I carried the crate outside, trying not to give myself a hernia in the process. I set down the crate in front of the scooter. Was this really how my elderly aunt got around town before her eyesight began to fail?

I fastened the crate to the basket with two black bungee cords I found in the shed. That ramshackle building was a treasure trove of seemingly useless items, as the police were discovering.

"As long as I don't hit any speed bumps, we should be good," I told the cat. She fixed her green eyes on me with a pleading expression and I couldn't discern whether it was the crate or the scooter that was the cause of her concern. Probably both. I got the impression that Ophelia liked roaming freely and didn't want to be tethered to anything.

I affixed the helmet to my head and heaved a sigh of resignation. I was about to discover whether helmet hair was a real thing.

I straddled the seat and started the scooter, hopeful that the weight of the crate didn't create too much of an imbalance. I wish I'd had more time to practice driving it before I placed another life in my hands. Granted, the ornery cat was probably fifty years old, but still.

How long did cats live? Another question for the vet.

Once I drove onto the main road, I tried to increase the speed, but the scooter seemed resistant.

Did this thing go over thirty miles per hour?

A pickup truck drove behind me, the driver beeping his horn. Thanks to the narrow and curvy nature of the road, this section was rightfully a no-passing zone. That being said, there was nothing I could do to go faster. I couldn't exactly floor it on a scooter.

He honked again, this time with more hostility. Part of me wanted to pull over and let him pass, despite the absence of a shoulder. The New Yorker in me, however, was a little more spiteful. I continued puttering along and ignored the urgent blare of the horn. His patience eventually wore out and he hit the gas. He made sure to flip me off as he passed me. I would've returned the gesture, but I was terrified of letting go.

Who said life was more laidback in the country?

I was relieved when I finally reached the vet's office. It was a short, squat red brick building with a decent-sized parking lot attached to it. I parked as close as I could get to the entrance. The fewer steps I had to lug the heavy crate, the better.

There was a young woman behind the counter with blue hair and a nose ring. "Can I help you?"

"Hi, I'm Mia Thorne and this is Ophelia." I tapped the crate with my foot, unwilling to lift it again. "We have an appointment with Dr. Warren."

The young woman behind the counter leaned over the counter for a look at the cat. "Hazel's Ophelia?"

"That's right."

She slid back into her chair and eyed me. "You've adopted Ophelia?"

"Sort of. Hazel was my dad's aunt. She left me her house and everything in it, including the cat."

She gave me an appraising look. "May the Force be with you."

That wasn't exactly encouraging. "You work at the vet's office. I thought you were supposed to like cats."

"I like cats the way parents love all their children equally."

I squinted at her. "I'm an only child so I don't know how to interpret that."

"You can go ahead back to the first room on the left," she said. "Dr. Warren will be with you in a few minutes."

"There's no concierge service?" I asked.

The blue-haired woman threw me a confused glance. "A what service?"

"No doorman? Bellhop? Someone to carry the crate to the room? To be honest, I was expecting someone to meet me outside."

She threw her head back and chortled. "That's a new one."

I looked down at the crate and heaved a sigh. If I threw my back out, I was withholding all future catnip as payback.

I bent with my knees like one of my former trainers taught me and shuffled to the exam room with the crate. I lowered the crate to the floor and slid it across the linoleum floor with my foot.

I dropped into a chair and glanced into the crate to check on Ophelia. Just because we weren't best friends didn't mean I wanted anything to be wrong with her. I wasn't a complete monster.

"How's it going in there?"

Ophelia hissed with a ferocity that made me jump. I straightened as a woman with light brown hair cut in a bob entered the room. I noticed that she wore protective gloves.

"Hello, I'm Dr. Warren. I understand you have Ophelia with you today."

"That's right. I'm Mia Thorne. Hazel was my father's aunt."

"We were so sorry to hear about her passing," Dr. Warren said. "She was a favorite here."

"She may have been, but I'm guessing not so much the cat."

Dr. Warren's smile was tight. "What brings you in today?"

"I need to get her tested for a bacterial disease. She bit me and scratched someone else and the woman she scratched has…" I struggled to remember the correct term. "Zoology disease."

"Zoonotic disease," Dr. Warren corrected me. She stooped down and opened the crate, prompting another hiss from Ophelia.

"Yes. They think it might be *Pasteurella multocida*." I pronounced the words carefully.

"Okay, we can run a test for that."

She lifted the cat and carried her to the exam table.

"Do you wear those gloves for all the animals?"

Dr. Warren smiled. "Only the most special ones."

"So, how old is Ophelia anyway?"

"We don't know for sure. Somewhere around twenty, we think. It's amazing that she's lived this long without too many complications, given her size."

I gazed at the volcano of a cat, her fur spread on the table like molten lava. "Should I put her on a diet or something?"

Dr. Warren laughed. "We've certainly recommended it over the years, but if Hazel wasn't successful, I'm not sure you're up to the task."

"Then you have no idea how much longer she might live?" I realized how awful that question must sound to the vet. I'd only just inherited her and already I was counting the days until I might be free of her.

Dr. Warren gave me a sympathetic look. "I understand it must be difficult for you. No experience with animals and suddenly you're thrust into a relationship with a particularly challenging cat. Ophelia knows her own mind, no doubt about that."

"I'm not sure why she bit me, to be honest. I was working in the garden and she just attacked."

Dr. Warren smiled. "She wanted your attention."

"Well, she got it." If it hadn't been for Ophelia biting me, I wouldn't have made the gruesome discovery.

The realization jolted me. I zoned out while Dr. Warren handled the cat with the help of an assistant, thinking about the cat tearing through the garden directly to the location of Gladys's body.

"All done, Miss Thorne," the vet said, breaking into my thoughts. "We'll let you know when get the results."

"Thanks." I paused. "So, I've been trying to get a picture of Aunt Hazel's life—friends and people she interacted with on a regular basis. Would you be any help with that?" It stood to reason that whoever killed Gladys had a connection to both the victim and Aunt Hazel, otherwise, why would they have been on the property in the first place?

Dr. Warren placed the cat back in the crate and locked the door. "I have a fairly limited viewpoint, but I can tell you that she only had two people here with Ophelia once she stopped driving on her own. One was her friend Gladys and one was her housekeeper."

"Housekeeper?" I repeated. It didn't occur to me that Aunt Hazel would've had a housekeeper. I'd wrongfully assumed that the help she rejected for the garden extended to the house.

"Well, more like a cleaning lady. Nothing fancy. Casey Schultz. I only know because Casey cleans my sister's house, too."

"Any idea where I can find her?"

"Not offhand, but I can get her number for you before you leave."

"Thanks, that would be great."

"You can take Ophelia to the front desk and I'll meet you out front."

I returned to the waiting area and Dr. Warren appeared a minute later with a slip of paper. "She drives around in a Ford Focus with the name of her company painted on the side, so if you see a bright blue car with 'Scrubs' written on it, that's her."

"Thanks for the tip." I tucked the number into my purse and the receptionist handed me the bill.

I nearly choked at the amount. "Holy cow. You know I only brought in one cat, right?" For this amount of money, it seemed like I should've brought in an entire litter.

The receptionist didn't flinch. "Will that be cash or credit?"

"Definitely credit." I dug into my purse and produced my wallet. "I thought you were supposed to increase your money with an inheritance, not lose it."

"Pets are expensive," the receptionist said matter-of-factly. "If you can't afford them, you shouldn't have them."

I gave her a sharp look. "Firstly, Ophelia is not a *pet*. She's a feline companion. Secondly, I didn't choose her, but she came with the house and I'm certainly not going to cast her out of the only home she's ever known." Red Clover was large enough for the both of us.

The receptionist dropped her gaze to the desk. "Sorry, I

didn't mean anything by it. It's just that I see a lot of folks adopting animals and then being surprised by the cost involved. Sometimes they end up giving the animal over to a shelter and it breaks my heart."

My gaze drifted to Ophelia curled up in the crate. What if I hadn't come to claim my inheritance? What would've happened to the aging and ornery cat? I couldn't imagine anyone would be quick to adopt her.

Some things were best not contemplated.

"No hard feelings," I said to the receptionist. "I totally understand where you're coming from." She probably saw a lot more than she cared to from her place at the vet's office, too.

She swiped the credit card through the machine, her lips forming a thin line. "I'm glad Ophelia found someone willing to take her on. She's not the easiest cat in the world."

"Well, I'm not the easiest woman in the world." Unless you spoke to my college boyfriend. Jay would have an entirely different opinion after one unfortunate incident involving his roommate and a bottle of tequila. In my defense, his roommate was a foreign exchange student to whom Jay insisted that I 'be nice.' Needless to say, the relationship didn't make it to graduation.

The bark of a dog drew my attention to the door. I was glad Ophelia was in the crate because she undoubtedly would've launched herself at the black and white Great Dane in a fight for dominance. I was so distracted by the dog that I failed to notice its owner.

"Mia?"

My chin jerked up into the Caribbean eyes of Dane Fairfax. He wore a classic grey suit with a white shirt and a black tie.

"Hi." I momentarily lost the power of speech at the sight of the handsome lawyer.

"I'm glad I ran into you. I heard about poor Gladys Spencer. Such bad luck."

"It's awful," the receptionist interjected. "Is Willow ready?"

"Your dog's name is Willow?" I asked. "She's beautiful."

He stroked the dog's back. "She certainly is." He handed the leash to the assistant who appeared in the waiting area.

"We'll have her back out to you in a few minutes," the assistant said and guided the dog into a back room.

"She's just here for a shot," Dane said. "Otherwise, I'd go back with her."

"Do you have a Great Dane because of your name?" I asked.

He laughed. "I don't know. Maybe that's what drew me to them initially, but Willow is a great dog."

"A gentle giant, right?"

"That's what they say."

"I saw your brother this morning," I said.

He flinched. "This morning?"

"The cops are searching my property," I quickly explained.

"Oh, right." He appeared to relax. "How are you settling in?"

"Outside of being a murder suspect, you mean? Not too bad." I opted not to mention the seance.

"Have you been cleared? My brother said the autopsy shows Gladys died before you came to town."

"I gave him the stub of my train ticket with the date I arrived."

"Good, good." He rocked back and forth on his heels and I felt like there was more he wanted to say. "Do you need help carrying the crate outside?"

"Would you mind? She's heavier than she looks." Who was I kidding? She was actually heavier than she looked.

"No problem." He bent down to lift the crate and I could see from his expression that he'd underestimated the weight.

I ran ahead to get the door for him and he settled the crate in the basket.

"You want me to do the bungee cords?" he asked. "I can basically do any kind of knot you need."

"Boy Scout?"

He offered a shy smile. "Made it all the way to Eagle Scout."

Naturally.

"Before you go, I was thinking maybe we could plan to get dinner one night this week. Help you sample the local fare."

My heart skipped a beat. "You're asking me out to dinner?"

"Is that…Yes." Dane seemed flustered.

"Yes, I would love that," I said.

I saw the relief flash in his eyes. "Great. How about tonight? I can pick you up at seven."

"What? You don't want ride together on my scooter?" I joked.

"I don't know. Maybe. I really like the way that helmet frames your face."

I laughed. "I haven't worked up the nerve to look in a mirror or I might never wear one again." I slipped the helmet on my head.

"Safety first," Dane said, patting the top of my helmet.

Warmth spread throughout my body in response to the unexpected affectionate gesture.

"I'll see you tonight," I said and drove away as fast as I could to keep myself from grinning at him like a lunatic.

CHAPTER ELEVEN

"Hard. No." Patrick stood in the doorway of my kitchen with his arms folded. "You cannot wear that on a date. You cannot wear those clothes I hate. You cannot wear that here or there. You cannot wear that anywhere."

I glanced at my outfit. "What's wrong with it, Dr. Seuss?"

"You look like a hooker with a heart of gold."

"Isn't that a good thing?"

"Maybe in the 90s. We're past that now." Patrick angled his head, scrutinizing me. "Dane Fairfax is a cerebral guy. He doesn't want too much skin."

I held out my arms to accentuate my three-quarter sleeves. "You think *this* is too much skin?"

"I can count your age spots." He paused. "Actually, I can't count your age spots because there are too many. You look like a dot-to-dot painting."

"Gee, thanks."

"I'm sorry, but I don't have time for sugarcoating. This is a sartorial emergency." He ushered me upstairs to my bedroom to change. "Let me see what I can find."

"No sweaters. They trigger hot flashes."

He ducked into the walk-in closet and groaned. "Are you sure you were living in New York City? These clothes scream Suburban White Woman."

"I like to blend in."

"Why would you want to do that?" He emerged from the closet holding two hangers. I recognized one dress from a former client's cocktail party and the other from Christmas Eve dinner a few years ago. I wasn't even sure that one would still fit me. I seemed to gain weight now by simply contemplating calories.

"You don't think those are too fancy?" I asked.

He blew a dismissive breath. "I know you think this is farmland, but Newberry is a very hip, eclectic town. Besides, Dane Fairfax is a catch. You need to glam it up if you want to lock him down."

"It's one date. I'm not locking down anything."

Patrick held out the black dress from the cocktail party. "Let me see you in this one. It's simple and chic."

"It's March. I'll freeze."

"Wear a jacket. You'll be fine. Didn't your mother ever teach you that we have to suffer for our art?"

"My mother taught me about suffering. Period."

Patrick's face split into a grin. "When is she coming? The more you talk about her, the more I can't wait to meet her."

"Sometime between this month and never." I took the hanger and hurried into the bathroom to change.

"You don't need to be modest," Patrick called.

"It's not modesty. It's embarrassment." My gym membership had been for access to the smoothie bar more than anything.

"I thought you had more confidence than that. My mistake."

I stripped off my clothes and started to pull the dress over my head, triggering a muscle spasm in my shoulder.

Crap.

Tears stung my eyes as the pain intensified.

Patrick knocked on the door. "Everything okay in there?"

"I'm stuck," I choked out.

He wedged the door open. "You're too muffled. What's going on?"

"My arms are stuck." I tried not to acknowledge his view of my apple stomach and unflattering underpants.

Patrick yanked down the fabric. "I'm glad this is a first date dress. You don't want to end up flailing like this in the bedroom later. On a sexiness scale, it's about a zero."

I massaged the offending muscle in my shoulder. "I think it's from carrying the cat's crate."

"I'm glad to see you already shaved your legs. We need to do something about your eyes. Do you have colored contacts?"

I bristled. "No, I only have reading glasses. What's wrong with my natural color?"

"They're hard to pin down. One second they're blue. Then they're green. Then grey. I don't know what to call them."

"And what? You think my lack of a clear eye color will put him off?"

"You want him gazing into your eyes because he's enchanted by you, not because he's trying to solve a mystery."

"I don't have contacts. I don't even like to wear eyeliner." I couldn't stand anything too close to my eyeball.

Patrick cupped my cheeks. "You are precious."

"I'm glad you think so. Let's hope Dane thinks so, too."

Dane arrived promptly at seven. Unsurprisingly, he looked just as amazing in casual clothes as he did in a suit.

"You look great."

"Thanks. So do you." I was relieved he didn't seem to think I was overdressed.

I walked to his idling Range Rover where he opened the passenger door for me.

"I noticed all the crime scene tape in your yard," he said, sliding into the driver's seat. "That's got to put a damper on moving into a new house."

"It isn't ideal, but I feel worse for Gladys." I made myself comfortable in the seat. "This is much better than a scooter."

He laughed as he pulled out of the driveway. "A big dog requires a big vehicle."

"You're pretty tall, too."

"Six-four. My brother hates that I have two inches on him."

I bit my tongue. It was much too early for tawdry talk.

He drove along River Road and into the heart of town. "I made reservations at Lark. Have you been there yet?"

"No, only Jama so far."

He parked on the street in front of a riverfront boutique hotel. "The ingredients here are mainly sourced from regional farmers."

"Sounds good to me."

The hostess seated us at an inside table overlooking the river. Outside was a pathway along the river illuminated by old-fashioned lampposts.

"I love the view," I said.

"Me, too," he said, smiling at me and I wondered if there was something in my teeth. Despite Patrick's warning, I'd eaten an apple earlier so that I didn't overeat at dinner.

I studied the impressive cocktail menu until I remembered that I wasn't supposed to drink while taking the amoxycillin. Bummer.

I ordered scallops and Dane ordered short ribs with a local IPA.

"My brother mentioned your arrest record."

I started to choke on my water. "What? Why would he do that?"

"What happened?"

"Nothing," I mumbled. "A youthful indiscretion."

"Well, we all have those."

I wasn't convinced Dane Fairfax had any. He seemed like a model citizen. He probably rinsed out all his recycling before putting it in the bin.

"I was upset that night. My boyfriend at the time, Bruce, had broken up with me and I'd gone out with friends. Needless to say, the evening didn't go as expected."

"Have you ever been married?" Dane asked.

"No. You?"

"Once," he said. "Lasted about five years."

"What happened?"

He shrugged. "We wanted different things. Grew apart. Nothing crazy."

"I was shocked when Bruce broke up with me. I'd already picked out my wedding gown. Our venue."

"You were engaged?"

"Oh, no. It was just that he was the first boyfriend where I actually pictured myself married, you know? I let myself believe in something for the first time in my life and then…it didn't happen." Nor did it happen with Andrew either. I was beginning to see a pattern.

"I'm sorry," Dane said, shaking his head, "but you couldn't have married him anyway."

"Why not?"

"Because his name was Bruce." He pulled a face. "You can't marry a guy called Bruce."

I laughed. "It wasn't the coolest name in the world, but love involves compromise. You and Derek got lucky in the name department."

"I don't know about that. Derek is a good name, but Dane's a little out there. I was named after my grandfather."

"That's nice. I was named after Amelia Earhart. My father wanted me to have the name of a positive female role model." I toyed with the napkin. "I think he'd be disappointed to learn I didn't become a pilot or something equally cool."

"He's…?"

"Dead. Yes. He died a long time ago, so you don't need to look so sad about it."

"It can still be sad. I get emotional whenever I think about my grandfather dying and I was only five at the time."

"You were close?" I was fascinated by people who were close with family members. I'd never been close to anyone in my family. My mother liked to hover and insert herself into my life, but she was too busy trawling for husbands to develop anything more than a superficial relationship with me.

"Yes, I think it bothered Derek that my grandfather doted on me, but we had a lot more in common. Derek was always on the go and I had more…academic interests."

"You were five when he died," I said. "What kind of academic interests did you have?"

"Dinosaurs. Insects. Aquatic life." He took a long sip of his beer. "Derek was more interested in pulling the wings off fireflies than learning about them."

After two glasses of water, my bladder signaled that it was time to get up. Although I hated to walk away in the middle of a good conversation, I didn't have a choice unless I wanted to impress Dane with my ability to make it rain under my chair.

I hustled down a narrow corridor to the restrooms. A familiar figure emerged from the men's room.

"Leo? No wait. Carlton."

He took a moment to register me. "New in town," he said, unsmiling. In fact, his whole demeanor was downcast.

"Mia," I reminded him. "Is everything okay?"

"Not really. My mom died unexpectedly. I'm at the bar commiserating with friends."

"I'm so sorry to hear that." Suddenly his last name sprang to mind—Carlton Spencer. "Your mom was Gladys," I blurted.

He frowned. "How do you know that?"

"She was found in my garden. *I* found her."

His eyes rounded. "Of course. I didn't make the connection. The police mentioned something about you, but I was too preoccupied to pay much attention. They asked me so many questions." He shook his head.

"It sucks, but I guess you're the obvious person to talk to if you have the most to gain from her death."

He dragged a hand through his hair. "I'm her next of kin, but I didn't inherit anything. My mom left everything to Kurt."

"Is that your brother?" I asked.

"No, my cousin. Kurt Wiggins."

My brow lifted. "That must've upset you."

Carlton pursed his lips. "No, man. Kurt's a guy in need of a handout. My mom knew I was doing fine on my own."

"So you knew about the will," I said. It was more of a statement than a question.

"Of course. Mom told me all about it. I guess she wanted to make sure I was cool with it."

"If Kurt was desperate for money, do you think...?" I left the question dangling between us.

Carlton blew a dismissive breath. "Kurt? Are you kidding? He's softer than my cashmere socks. No way would he have the stomach for something like that. Plus, he loved my mom. She doted on him like he was her own son."

"Still, if he's the only one who stands to gain anything from her death..."

"Maybe it was a random attack," Carlton said.

"Maybe." Although it seemed unlikely. She wasn't mugged or violated.

"Anyway, I'm trying to stay out of their way and let them investigate," he said. "I'd like to put this whole thing behind me."

"You're a more patient person than I am. Speaking of which, I really need to go." I motioned to the restroom.

"If you want to join us after dinner, we'll still be at the bar."

"Thanks, but I'm on a date." I didn't think Dane would welcome the suggestion to meet a group of other men at the bar afterward.

I finished in the restroom and returned to the table wearing a fresh coat of lipstick. My mother would be proud.

"I just ran into the victim's son," I said. "He's over at the bar. Talk about awkward." I spotted Leo and Jax with him and immediately registered the bandage on Jax's hand. He'd been wearing it at Jama, too. I looked at the bandage on my own hand. Jax had blamed the injury on something in the office, but what if...? No, that made no sense. What motive could he possibly have?

Dane followed my gaze to the bar. "My brother mentioned they're interested in the nephew. Apparently he doesn't have an alibi for the time of the murder and Derek got the distinct impression the guy is hiding something."

"Um, that would be *a murder*," I said. "He's hiding a murder."

"Not necessarily. Anyway, the police don't have enough evidence to make it stick. They're still trying to find the murder weapon."

"And in the meantime, the nephew wanders free?" I asked. "That doesn't seem right."

"You were walking around free when they suspected you," Dane reminded me.

"Yes, but I am innocent," I emphasized the last word.

He leaned forward wearing a seductive expression. "Yes, but how innocent?"

I licked my lips, my pulse racing. "What do you have in mind?"

"Dessert," Dane said, eyeing a passing tray of sweets.

Right, he meant food. Of course he did. "I am open to suggestions."

We ended up sharing the chocolate lava cake and it was way hotter than the spaghetti scene in *Lady and the Tramp*, mostly because it involved cake.

After dinner, we ambled along the pathway and admired the moonlight's reflection on the water. The walk was both romantic and good for digestion. A win-win.

"This has been fun," he said. "I hope we can do it again sometime."

I looked up at him to respond and the back of my neck began to tingle. An image flashed in my mind of Dane kissing me in front of the door at Red Clover. I threw a hand against a lamppost to steady myself.

Dane studied me. "Mia? Are you okay?"

I was so surprised by my vision that I didn't know what to say. "Yes, just a dizzy spell. Sorry. I had a great time, too."

He appeared unconvinced, not that I blamed him. I must've stared at him like a dead fish. If it had been a daydream, I wouldn't have been so freaked out, but it wasn't. It felt more like a memory of something that hadn't happened yet.

"I'm pretty worn out," I said. "Would you mind driving me home now?"

"Of course."

We chatted easily on the drive home, and Dane mentioned a few historical facts about buildings we passed. By the time he pulled in front of Red Clover, I'd almost forgotten the strange moment.

Almost.

"Good night, Dane. Thank you."

I escaped from the car before he could walk me to the door. As much as I wanted to kiss him, I also didn't want the vision—or whatever it was—to be true. The implications would be too much to digest. Part of me thought I was overreacting. It was probably anticipation. The date had gone well and it was only natural that I could see him kissing me at my front door.

I unlocked the door and slipped inside. I leaned against the door with my heart pounding, feeling simultaneously relieved and disappointed.

"Leave it to me to screw up the best date I've had in years," I said.

Ophelia's green eyes appeared in the darkness and I switched on the light.

"I guess you're here to make things worse."

The cat sauntered toward me and rubbed her side against my leg. I remained perfectly still, afraid that if I moved, she'd bite me. It was only when I heard the soft purring sound that I realized I was safe. I bent down and cautiously placed a hand on her back to pet her. Ophelia meowed and shifted to rub her head against the palm of my hand.

"I stand corrected," I whispered.

CHAPTER TWELVE

It appeared to be toddler hour at the library. An entire section of the building seemed devoted to corralling wandering little ones who were disinterested in story time.

Although I'd applied online for a library card, you have to show up in person with two forms of identification in order to receive it, so Scarlet kindly offered to drive me.

"There's a new gardening book I want to check out," Scarlet said.

"I can't imagine anything more boring than reading a book about plants."

She cut a sideways look at me. "I think you'd find it extremely helpful."

"I'll rely on you and the internet, as soon as the police give me the all-clear to return to the garden."

Scarlet clutched my arm. "Great Goddess, it's Kurt Wiggins."

I followed her gaze to a thin man in a brown leather jacket perusing one of the fiction aisles. His hair was so thin that I could see his scalp beneath it.

"That's Gladys's nephew?"

She nodded. "I can't believe the police suspect him. He's always seemed so sweet to me."

"I want to talk to him," I said.

Scarlet's eyes widened. "Why? Let the police handle it."

"Because he'll be off his guard with me. He doesn't know who I am. Maybe he'll slip up and say something I can share with Detective Fairfax." And maybe I would sleep better knowing a killer was no longer on the loose.

Scarlet nudged me. "Maybe you just want more time with the hot detective. His brother isn't enough for you."

My cheeks flamed as I remembered my vision of Dane kissing me. If only it hadn't unsettled me so much. With my luck, I'd never hear from Dane again.

"Stay here. I'm going to see what I can find out."

I studied Kurt for a moment, pretending he was a prospective client I wanted to land for the paper. I had a few tactics I generally employed when it came to charming strangers and Kurt Wiggins seemed ripe for the Friendly Woman Who Might Eventually Bang Me technique.

I wandered over to the aisle and glimpsed the selection of titles in front of him. Kurt's hand hovered in front of a Nicholas Sparks book and he seemed uncertain whether he wanted to take a closer look.

"I wouldn't touch that one unless you have an ample supply of tissues," I said.

Kurt's hand dropped to his side. "I'm in the mood for a tear-jerker, though. You might have just convinced me." He met my gaze. "Let me know if you need help finding anything."

"You work here?"

"Part-time. I don't usually work today, but I had to call out yesterday."

No kidding. "Really? Why is that?"

"My aunt died," he said glumly.

I slapped my cheek. "You're kidding? Mine, too."

Kurt laughed awkwardly. "If this were a rom-com, they'd call this a meet cute." He paused. "Except for the part about the dead aunts."

"Yeah, that's pretty morbid. Maybe a dark comedy?" I offered helpfully. "Such a tragedy. My aunt's death was sudden and unexpected." Despite her advanced age and failing health.

Kurt's eyes teared up. "Same."

"Were you two close?" I asked.

His head bobbed up and down. "We were. That's why I'm looking for a Nicholas Sparks book, actually. He was one of her favorite authors. I thought I would honor her memory by reading one."

I swallowed hard. This guy didn't seem like a killer, unless his choice of Nicholas Sparks was motivated by guilt rather than a genuine desire to honor his late aunt.

"That's incredibly sweet," I said. "My aunt was a big fan of John Grisham." It wasn't necessarily a lie. I'd spotted a copy of *The Firm* on a shelf in the cottage—covered in dust.

Someone shushed me from across the room. I turned to see the librarian glaring at me.

Kurt ducked his head and chuckled. "Mrs. Linsky takes her job very seriously."

"I noticed." I leaned against the shelf, affecting a casual air. "It's a strange twist of fate that my aunt was such a fan of crime thrillers in light of her murder."

Kurt started to choke and I whacked him on the back. "Your aunt was murdered?" he asked in disbelief.

"I know. Crazy, right? I mean, people get murdered every day, but you never think it will happen to someone you know."

Kurt stared at me with an awestruck expression. "My aunt was murdered, too."

I took a careful step backward. "Okay, this is getting bizarre. How?"

He shook his head. "I don't know. The police are investigating. They thought it might be some transient, but they ruled her out."

Transient? I squelched my desire to defend myself. "That's terrible. What happened?" I noticed he didn't mention his own potential involvement.

"Aunt Gladys was found in a friend's garden. At first, they thought she fell and hit her head, but now they think someone deliberately hit her."

I clutched the strap of my purse against my chest in mock horror. "In a small town like this? Can you imagine?"

"Aunt Gladys was the nicest lady in the world. I don't know why anyone would want to hurt her."

"Any idea what she was doing alone in her friend's garden?" I asked.

"I think she was on her way to feed the cat. The friend passed away a couple months ago and they've been waiting to hear from a distant relative. Aunt Gladys was broken up about it. She and Hazel spent a lot of time together."

I pulled *The Notebook* off the shelf and handed it to him. "Read this one."

"You think?"

"I do think."

"I wish I could stop thinking," he mused. "Now that Aunt Gladys is gone, I need to decide whether to break the lease on my apartment. All these big decisions I wasn't expecting to make."

"Why would you do that?"

"Because Aunt Gladys left me her house." He paused for a breath. "She left me everything."

What was it with elderly aunts leaving their houses to nieces and nephews?

"She didn't have any kids of her own?" I asked, feigning ignorance.

"She has a son, but my cousin does well for himself. Always has. She didn't worry about him."

I gave him a sidelong look. "But she worried about you?"

"All the time. Too much, probably." He shook his head. "She doesn't have to worry now. Between her life insurance policy and the house, I'll be in good shape for the rest of my life. It doesn't make up for her loss, but I have to admit, the stress relief is a welcome change."

Kurt Wiggins inherited Gladys's house *and* the proceeds of her life insurance policy?

"Talk about motive," I blurted. Oops. Didn't mean to say that out loud.

Kurt rubbed the back of his neck, smiling awkwardly. "Yeah, Carlton said the same thing."

"Carlton?"

"My cousin, Carlton Spencer. We're as close as brothers. We spent all our time together as kids."

"Must've been a lot of fun." I would've liked a constant companion instead of inventing imaginary friends.

Kurt's expression grew dreamy. "Our childhood was pretty idyllic. Aunt Gladys made sure of that. I owe her a great deal."

"It's probably a good thing you can offer an alibi for the time of death." It was a terrible segue, but I wanted to raise the topic before he wandered away.

Kurt's expression clouded over. "Um, yeah. Unfortunately, I can't give them one." Tears slid down his cheek and I fumbled through my purse for a clean tissue.

"Here you go."

He wiped away the tears. "Sorry about that. I'm such a mess. The whole business has me rattled pretty good."

"I can imagine. I'm so sorry." I glanced over my shoulder

to see Scarlet peering at us from behind a stack of books. "I should get going. It was nice to meet you. Good luck with everything."

"Hey, what did you say your aunt's name was?"

"Jemima," I said, and instantly regretted the choice.

His brow lifted. "Wow. That's not a name you hear every day."

"She was from England."

"Oh." He held up *The Notebook*. "I'm going to check this out at the end of my shift. Thanks for the suggestion."

"Don't mention it," I said, turning away. Seriously don't mention it. I couldn't stand Nicholas Sparks' books.

I collected my library card and checked out a Janet Evanovich book. My mind lingered on Kurt's response about the alibi. Something about the phrasing bothered me. He didn't say *I don't have one*. Instead, he'd said *I can't give them one*. It reminded me of clients who wanted to purchase a premium ad but only had the money for a half page. They would never come right out and admit the cost was out of their budget. They had to hide any potential financial issues, so they came up with statements like *we can't fit it into the ad schedule this quarter*.

"Well?" Scarlet prompted as we exited the library.

"Carlton was right," I said. "No way did that guy kill his aunt."

Scarlet dropped me off at the end of the driveway. As I approached Red Clover, I spotted an unfamiliar car ahead of me. My gaze shifted to the figure on my doorstep. I immediately yanked out my phone in case I needed to call for help. There was no sign of the police or their crime scene tape. They seemed to have packed up and left.

"Hello?" I called from a safe distance.

The figure turned to face me. The woman was five and a half feet tall with red hair and the fashion sense of Krystle Carrington from *Dynasty*. It wouldn't surprise me to learn that she wore a sequined bathrobe with a fur collar around the house.

"I'm Mimi Van Haren," the woman said. "Are you Hazel's replacement?"

Replacement? That was a funny word for relative.

I inched closer to the doorstep. "I'm Mia Thorne."

Her shoulders relaxed. "A Thorne. I thought as much. I was a regular of Hazel's."

I wore a blank expression. "A regular what?"

"Client."

I didn't realize she had a job outside taking care of her own gardens. "What did Aunt Hazel do for you?" I asked, genuinely curious.

Mimi smiled at me. "Whatever I needed. Tarot card readings, palm readings, love potions."

"Oh, wow. I had no idea." I clearly needed to take a closer look at the contents of the house.

"She was officially retired, but she still made time for a select few." Mimi flashed a smile. "And I was one of them."

"You knew her well?"

"About thirty years," Mimi said. "I moved here from Ohio with my first husband and, when we divorced, he moved away and I stayed. Newberry became the home I'd been searching for."

"That's nice," I said. I'd never really known that feeling. I was comfortable in the city, of course, but I wouldn't say anyplace I'd lived had truly felt like home.

"What's your specialty?" Mimi asked.

"Bourbon sour is a new favorite," I said.

Mimi laughed. "Not specialty cocktail. Your specialty." She gave me a meaningful look.

"Um, I'm not sure."

"Do you read tarot cards? Offer a voodoo doll service?"

"There's a service?"

"I'm in the market for a new man," Mimi said. "I broke things off with my latest and not-so-greatest and I'd like a replacement."

Now it was my turn to laugh. "You're talking about a man, not a battery."

"Lots of similarities there," Mimi said.

"Well, I'm afraid I don't know how to read cards. I barely play cards." I learned to play rummy and Go Fish when I was a kid, but that was the extent of my card knowledge.

"That's a shame." Mimi scrutinized me. "You should learn. There's money to be made here for someone with your skill."

"My skill currently involves dodging a murder rap, so I don't know that I'd have energy left over for mining untapped potential."

Mimi splayed a hand against her chest. "Oh, I heard about poor Gladys Spencer. Such a tragedy." She hesitated. "I wonder if I can get her German potato salad recipe now. She always said I could have it over her dead body."

"I understand Gladys and my aunt were good friends," I said.

"Oh, yes. They were thick as thieves, those two. I didn't tend to see Hazel socially, mostly for professional reasons."

"Well, I'm sorry I can't help you out. Maybe try a dating app. I hear they're pretty good."

She wrinkled her nose. "No thank you. I put my faith in magic, not technology." She reached into her purse and produced a business card. "If you change your mind, give me a call."

"Thanks. I will." I resisted the urge to laugh at the thought of me conducting readings. I pictured me in Patrick's turban and snorted.

Mimi returned to her car, checking her teeth in the reflection of the window before opening the door. "You should really do something about the jungle in the yard," she called. "Hazel might come back from the dead if she finds out what a state it's in."

I didn't have the heart to tell her that if Gladys didn't come back to identify her murderer, I seriously doubted Hazel would return to complain about a bunch of dead plants.

As I entered the cottage, my phone rang and I recognized the vet's number.

"Hello?"

"Hi, this is Dr. Warren's office. We just want to let you know that your cat tested positive for *Pasteurella multocida.*"

Instinctively, I scanned the interior for Ophelia, but she was nowhere to be seen. The assistant explained next steps and I tried to take in everything she said, but my head was spinning. Although I knew Ophelia wasn't responsible for Gladys's death, I hated the idea that the cat had attacked her in her final moments. After all, Gladys was only here to feed the cat.

I began searching the house for the cat to deliver the news. If she recognized the name Hazel, maybe the cat would also recognize *Pasteurella multocida.* It was worth a shot.

There was no sign of her inside, so I exited the kitchen door and across the deck, passing through the so-called witch's garden.

"Ophelia, where are you?"

My gaze swept the area and I noticed a familiar figure in a kayak on the river. I sauntered to the water's edge.

"Hey, Chief Tuck," I said, waving.

The older man wore a blue visor and gripped a fishing rod. When he didn't respond, I wondered if I hadn't been loud enough. I inched closer to the water and yelled his name again, waving my arms more dramatically.

He leveled me with a look. "Pipe down, woman. Are you trying to scare away all the fish?"

I scanned the surface of the water. "Could I really do that?"

"Fishing is meant to be relaxing. How relaxing do you think it is when someone's yelling and waving their arms like they're about to drown?"

I put my hands on my hips. "I guess you're not in the mood for company then."

"The only company I'm interested in has scales and gills."

"Must be nice to have a hobby," I said. "I'll bet you need a distraction from all the murder solving." I snapped my fingers. "Oh, wait. You haven't solved the murder yet."

Chief Tuck glared at me. "If you must know, we'll be making an arrest shortly. In fact, Detective Fairfax is probably making it as we speak."

What a relief. "Who?"

"The victim's nephew, Kurt Wiggins."

Energy pulsed through my body.

"No, that isn't right. Kurt didn't kill his aunt," I said.

Chief Tuck continued fishing, as though we were discussing the weather. "And how do you know that?"

"Because."

"That's very persuasive Ms. Thorne, but not as persuasive as no alibi, opportunity, and motive."

"What's your evidence?"

"How about the murder weapon? Does that suit you?"

Yikes. "What was it?"

"We found Kurt's baseball bat discarded in that jungle of yours. Has his fingerprints all over it, as well as his aunt's DNA."

The back of my neck tingled. "He didn't do it," I yelled before I could stop myself.

"Unless you know something we don't, seems like an open-and-shut case."

Ugh. Why did I still believe Kurt was innocent? It would be so much easier to let it go. I was out of the running now. Let the police handle it. Kurt will hire a good lawyer and have a solid defense.

No, he wouldn't. Kurt wouldn't be able to afford a good lawyer without his aunt's money and he wouldn't be able to collect the money if he was charged with her murder.

"You might as well know that the cat tested positive for that bacteria," I said.

Something tugged on his fishing line. "Figured she would. Thanks for letting me know."

"I guess it doesn't make any difference to the case."

"Don't see why it should."

I turned back toward the house, feeling despondent. I couldn't explain why I thought Kurt was innocent. I certainly had no evidence. Maybe I was right the first time—maybe the thing Kurt was hiding was his guilt. It seemed absurd to think he was hiding something that could exonerate him. What could be so important that he couldn't tell the police?

I stomped into the house with one goal in mind—to find the real killer of Gladys Spencer. I may not have had a job in ad sales anymore, but I still had the skills that made me semi-successful. Persistence was the key, Lynette always said, and so persistent I intended to be.

CHAPTER THIRTEEN

Patrick's house was only two doors down from mine, also positioned on the riverbank. With its large windows and green siding with dark red trim, the Victorian house was chock full of what HGTV would call 'old world charm.' A plaque on the fence identified the house's origin as 1885.

As I knocked on the door, I noticed the doormat under my feet read *Go Away* in block letters. Despite the message, my phone lit up with a text from Patrick—*come in*. I opened the door and stepped into the spacious foyer, inhaling the intermingled scents of cinnamon and citrus.

Upstairs, he texted. *First room on left.*

I headed to the staircase, noting a piano on full display in the living room. The sight of the instrument didn't surprise me. There was no way Patrick managed to play the way he did without practice.

In the designated room, Patrick sat at a vanity table, applying thick black liner to each eye.

"Are you baking?" I asked. "Something smells delicious."

"Oh, no. It's a candle."

I let my gaze wander around Patrick's black and white

bedroom. It was an interesting mix of design elements, including black and white framed photographs on the wall and a dramatic black chandelier hanging over the bed.

"Thanks for inviting me tonight," I said. "It'll be nice to take my mind off Gladys for a few hours."

"Yes, nobody deserves to be haunted by the image of a murdered old woman." He paused. "Well, I guess there are a few people I can think of who deserve it, but not you." He turned to offer a faint smile.

"That's some serious eye makeup," I said.

Patrick admired his reflection in the mirror. "I always like to dress professionally for the full moon. Show some respect."

I peered at him curiously. "Because that's when you…turn?"

He applied a coat of gloss to his lips. "Yes, one night a month I turn heterosexual."

"It's when he performs his cleansing ritual," Scarlet said, appearing in the bedroom doorway.

Patrick fluffed his hair. "It demands my best."

"And that includes the best eye makeup?" I asked.

He shot me a puzzled look. "Naturally."

"If you're going to wash away negative energy, you might as well look good doing it," Scarlet added.

"Negative energy?" I queried. "What happened? Your mother called?"

A brief smile touched his pouty lips. "I like my mom."

"Then what?"

Patrick offered a cavalier shrug. "Haunted objects. Paranormal activity. I strip away the unwanted energy and restore items to their former glory."

I wasn't sure how to respond. "Like a Ghostbuster?"

"Not quite," he said.

"And people pay you in legal currency for this?" I asked.

"Occasionally I'm willing to barter," Patrick said. "Sofia Milano owns a store with amazing vintage finds and her access to inventory is worth far more than a personal check."

"What is it that you cleanse?" I pictured him stripping naked and wading into the moonlit river with a bar of soap and a washcloth.

Patrick's lips curved into a smile. "I'll show you."

Scarlet and I followed him down the hallway until we reached a smaller room at the far end of the house. He flung open the door with gusto.

"This is the room of treasures," he announced. "Some of these I chose not to cleanse."

I surveyed the room and noted several paintings, a random assortment of rocking chairs, and a creepy doll with shining eyes that seemed to stare into my very soul. I shivered involuntarily.

"And they're haunted?" I asked.

Patrick arched his perfect eyebrow. "Does that scare you?"

I examined one of the wooden rocking chairs. It looked pleasant enough, like a lovely old woman had wiled away the hours in that chair, knitting and chatting about her children and grandchildren.

"Not necessarily. How does it work? Is this room filled with ghosts all competing for attention?"

"Not exactly," Patrick said. "These spirits are attached to their respective items."

"Then why keep them? Why not cleanse them?"

"Because these spoke to me," he said.

"I thought they all they spoke to you. Isn't that part of being a ghost whisperer?"

"I don't mean literally speak to me," he huffed. "I mean I feel a sense of peace, like I have a bond with the spirits that occupy them. If I cleanse them, I'll lose that connection."

I frowned at the creepy doll. "How does that thing give you a sense of peace? It looks like it wants to stab me in my sleep."

"First of all, that *thing* has a name."

"Malachi?" I ventured and Scarlet bit down on her lip to keep from laughing.

"Her name is Susie." Patrick plucked the doll from the chair and hugged it to his chest. "It's not the doll itself. It's the vibe I get from it."

"The vibe to murder without mercy?" I folded my arms. "Where was Susie on the day of the murder?"

Patrick kissed the doll's forehead and returned her to the chair. "Susie doesn't walk on her own."

"Says you."

"If Susie was prone to murder, she would've started with someone like Jack Delancey."

"Who's Jack Delancey?"

"The know-it-all who hangs out in the coffee shop dispensing unwelcome wisdom. She hates guys like that."

"Well, I can hardly blame her for that." I sucked in a breath. "Yeah, still creepy from where I'm standing, though." I inched away in case it decided to go full poltergeist. "When did you learn you could do this?"

"Pretty early on. My grandparents had a portrait of my great-grandmother in their house. It was one of those paintings where the eyes follow you and everyone else in my family was afraid of it."

"Then why keep it out to watch everyone?"

Patrick pulled a face. "Because they were too afraid of her ghost to put it in storage. Apparently, she was a formidable woman."

"Those are always the ones to stick around, aren't they? You never hear about some meek and feeble ghost haunting anywhere. They're either sticking their tongue in your ear when you're in the bathroom or throwing your breakables around the house."

Scarlet's upper lip curled. "What ghost sticks its tongue in your ear?"

Patrick clasped his hands in prayer form. "Yes, do tell so I can put it on my bucket list."

"Some haunted restaurant in Savannah, I think. The ghost of a perverted gentleman that accosts women in the restroom," I said. That being said, I'd gotten pretty drunk on Southern cocktails in that restaurant so it could've been an actual pervert that followed me into the bathroom.

"Sadly, there are no pervert ghosts in this house," Patrick said. He pointed at his collection. "The rocking chair is Frieda. The painting of the dog is Gerald."

"Should I be taking notes?" I asked. One would think I was good at remembering names given my career as a salesperson. One would be wrong.

Patrick ignored me. "Everyone, this is my new friend, Mia Thorne. I expect you all to be nice to her." He waited for a beat. "She's the great-niece of Hazel. You remember her?"

I tapped my cheek. "Is it great-niece or grand-niece? I can never remember."

Scarlet shrugged.

"Now we have to gather what I need for the ritual and we can head outside," Patrick said.

"I'll get the bottle of wine and the glasses," Scarlet said.

"None for me, thanks," I said.

"The prosecco is in the fridge," he called after her.

I locked eyes with the doll and shivered. "Are the items you need in this room?"

"Yes, but it will only take a minute. I try to keep everything organized. Don't want to accidentally cleanse the wrong object."

"Has that ever happened?"

"Once or twice. That's why I stick to light alcohol now before a ritual."

He pulled an empty crate from underneath a console table and started to place items inside. A clock. An urn. A small statute of a head with its eyes closed.

"Would you mind grabbing that bag?" he asked, pointing to a tote bag.

I went to lift it and realized it was already full of stuff. "What's in here?"

"Candles, rocks, and a few other things I use." Once the crate was filled, he started toward the doorway. "You can follow me. I'll show you where we're setting up camp."

We exited the house via the back door and walked along a stone path toward the river. Patrick stopped about halfway and set the crate on the lawn.

"Scarlet will bring the blanket and booze," he said.

I watched the sun dip below the tree line, creating a deep pink backdrop.

"Looks like the world is burning," I remarked.

"Sometimes it feels that way, too," Patrick said.

"I know that feeling," I murmured.

He cocked his head. "Anything you want to talk about?"

I waved him off. "No thanks. Some things are best left alone, like that portrait with the formidable lady."

"Why do I get the distinct impression that somebody did you wrong?"

My jaw tightened. "Who hasn't been done wrong at least once in their lifetime? I'm not special."

"I think you're more special than you realize," Patrick said.

I heard a hooting sound from outside. "Is that an actual owl?"

"No, it's the nature app on my phone. Of course it's an actual owl." Patrick shook his head. "City people."

I listened for the hooting sound again. It was much cooler than the sound of the cross-street bus with the added bonus of no eye-level commuters peeking in my bathroom window, which was the situation I found myself in when I lived on the second floor of an apartment building.

Scarlet approached us, carrying a large wicker basket. The bottle of prosecco and two flute glasses were nestled on top of a folded blanket. She set the basket on the ground next to the crate and Patrick unfurled the softest-looking blanket I'd ever seen.

"Is that sheepskin?" I asked.

He rubbed the material against his cheek. "No. It's faux fur, not that you'd know by the price tag. But I splurged because it's a business expense."

"It's not a business expense," Scarlet murmured.

"The internet told me," Patrick shot back.

"The internet also told you that you could eliminate ass pimples by using rubbing alcohol on them," she said. "And how did that work out for you?"

Patrick straightened the corners of the blanket with extra zeal. "We swore we'd never speak of that again."

Scarlet seemed to know what to do next without being told. She gathered materials from the crate and began to create a circle on the ground, alternating between candles and rocks.

"What's up with the clock?" she asked.

"Bad juju," Patrick replied. "The owners said unpleasant things started to happen after they brought it home from Switzerland."

"Ooh, it's like the monkey's paw," I said.

"No, you don't make wishes on the clock," Patrick corrected me.

"So you cleanse it and give the clock back?" I asked.

"That's what they pay me for." He set the clock in the circle.

I scrutinized the clock. It was nondescript as far as clocks went. "What kind of bad things?"

"The husband lost his job. The wife was diagnosed with cancer. A few other unfortunate events."

I backed away from the circle. "And they think it's the clock?"

"Everything was going really well for them until this thing showed up." Patrick shrugged. "They think the clock is the culprit."

"Why not get rid of it instead of cleansing it?" Who needs an old-fashioned clock when you have a phone anyway?

"They bought it together on a trip for their twentieth wedding anniversary," he said. "It has sentimental value."

I couldn't imagine caring about an object that much. Then again, I wasn't very sentimental. Even the photos of my dad were stored in a box. I didn't like the idea of having his image in view on a daily basis. I felt like I was constantly disappointing him as it was—to be subjected to his face would be a bridge too far.

"How much do you get paid for this?" I asked.

"Depends on the item," he said. "Some items are too big to travel, so I have to make a house call. That costs more because I have to do the ritual in the home."

"And you make a living from this?" It seemed hard to believe.

"I won't be buying a Porsche anytime soon, but I do well enough."

"I won't be buying a car anytime soon," I said. "Forget about a Porsche."

"I love that you're driving around on Hazel's scooter," Scarlet said. "I think your aunt would get a kick out of it."

"It's better than the subway, I'll say that much." It was nice to be traveling around in fresh air without the stench of body odor or the wandering gaze of a lecherous commuter.

Scarlet lit the candles and Patrick took his place in the center of the circle, sitting cross-legged.

"We stay out here?" I asked.

Scarlet nodded. "You don't want to interfere with the circle or you'll disrupt the ritual."

I held up my hands. "Definitely not." I wouldn't want to do that and risk letting loose an evil spirit. I'd seen *Ghostbusters* half a dozen times.

The clock and other items were now bathed in moonlight.

"We're charging these with lunar energy," Patrick explained.

More like looney energy, but I kept that to myself.

"The water and the moon provide an effective cleanse," he continued.

"Do we have to chant or something?" I asked.

"Not for this," he said. "We let nature take its course." He smoothed back his hair and raised the clock toward the sky, closing his eyes in the process.

I leaned over to Scarlet and whispered, "How much of this is real and how much is performance art?"

"It's about fifty-fifty," she whispered back. "Patrick leans into drama like nobody else."

Patrick repeated the exercise with each item on the blanket until they'd all been bathed in moonlight.

"You do this every full moon?" I asked.

"Like clockwork," he said. He patted the top of the clock. "No pun intended."

"If there's a special moon like a blood moon or a blue moon, he'll take advantage of that, too," Scarlet added.

"How do you know you were successful?" I asked, glancing at the items.

Patrick touched the top of the clock. "I can sense it."

"And what if their luck doesn't change?" I asked. "Will they ask for a refund?"

"It's happened on occasion, but generally people are happy with my services." He stretched onto the blanket and gazed at the darkened sky.

Scarlet sighed contentedly. "I love nights like this. Seeing the full moon and the stars...It reminds me of how connected I am to the universe. That I'm a part of something bigger than myself."

Patrick tucked his hands behind his head. "I like the way my skin glows in starlight." He turned his head to look at me and touched his cheek. "It looks nice, right? Very Ingrid Bergman."

"Beautiful," I agreed.

Patrick shifted to rest on his elbow and observe me. "If we're going to be friends, there are a few basic questions we need to get out of the way."

I cocked an eyebrow. "Such as?"

"Favorite Chris?"

"Hemsworth," I said without hesitation.

"Chris Pine for me," Scarlet said.

"Come on, you two. It's clearly Evans," Patrick said. "Have you seen that GIF where he rips a piece of wood into two pieces?"

I snorted. "I guess I've failed the test then?"

"You didn't say Pratt, so you're okay." Patrick patted my arm reassuringly.

"I miss spending lazy time outside," I said. "When I was a kid, I used to play Winnie-The-Pooh with my dad. He'd be Tigger and I'd be Pooh and we'd walk through the yard and pretend it was the Hundred Acre Wood." I smiled at the memory of my energetic father bouncing on his toes. He was great at playing pretend.

"No Piglet?" Scarlet asked.

"My mom didn't like to play and she certainly wouldn't have been Piglet." My mother had an aversion to anything that involved imagination. She used to chastise me for reading too much and filling my head with nonsense. My babysitter used to call me Matilda, after the girl in the Roald Dahl book.

"What is Winnie-the-Pooh, anyway?" Patrick asked.

I stared at him. "Are you high? He's a bear."

"Then why not call him Winnie-the-Bear? His name makes him sound like some kind of emo poop."

"You're the only one who's emo around here," Scarlet said.

"Did you ever play imaginative games when you were younger?" I asked.

"I played dress-up," Patrick said.

Scarlet snorted. "Shocker."

"Did it freak out your parents?" I asked.

"Not at all," he said. "My dad was the one who used to paint my nails and my mom bought me whatever style clothes I wanted. They weren't into setting limits."

Wow. What was it like to have a supportive parent?

Movement in the shadows caught my eye and I jumped. "There's an animal stalking us," I said quickly. "What if it's rabid?"

Scarlet peered into the darkness. "It's Ophelia."

"Ophelia?" I squinted for a better look at the potential threat. Sure enough, I recognized the very oval silhouette of the oversized cat. "What's she doing here?"

"She's nosy," Patrick said. He urged the cat closer so he could pet her.

"Does she spend a lot of time over here?" I asked.

"She's drawn to rituals," he replied. "I think she senses when something interesting is happening."

"Or she's stalking me."

Scarlet observed the cat. "She's the one who let us know that Hazel had died."

I raised my eyebrows at the cat. "Really?"

Scarlet nodded. "She came scratching at Patrick's door and meowing uncontrollably."

I felt a pang of sadness as I pictured the anxious cat delivering the bad news.

"At least she went peacefully," I said, which was more than I could say for Gladys.

"It was her time," Scarlet said. "She was ready."

"I wish I was," I said. Although the opportunity to come here arose when I needed it most, I still felt unprepared for a life in Newberry, no matter how temporary.

"You've made a few handsome gentlemen friends since your arrival," Patrick said. "That must help."

I blushed. "I don't know about that."

"Dane Fairfax seems to want to make your acquaintance," Scarlet said.

I waved a hand. "Oh, I'm sure I messed that up already."

Patrick idly plucked a blade of grass from the ground. "Too bad. He's got pecs that would make Chris Evans weep with envy."

I sat up straighter. "Really?"

Scarlet smiled. "Only because Patrick has seen him kayaking in the summer."

"Who kayaks without a shirt?" I asked.

"A guy with pecs like Dane Fairfax, apparently," Scarlet said. "If you've got 'em, flaunt 'em."

"I saw Chief Tuck kayaking," I said. "Not quite the same experience."

They laughed.

"Don't be fooled," Scarlet said. "He was a looker in his day. I've seen photos."

"Oh, I believe it." I glanced at the pile of cleansed objects. "I wish there was a way to cleanse all my mistakes."

"I'm sure Kurt wishes the same thing about now," Patrick said.

"He didn't kill her," I said. If anyone would be willing to take my unsubstantiated claim to heart, it was these two.

"I'd agree with you, but from what you told us, you have to admit the evidence is pretty damning," Patrick said.

I scratched the back of my neck, remembering the tingling sensation I'd felt earlier. "I can't explain why, but I know Kurt is innocent."

"I believe you," Patrick said softly.

Scarlet shuddered and hugged herself. "Which means the real killer is still out there."

CHAPTER FOURTEEN

THE NEXT MORNING on my way through town, I spotted a bright blue car parked outside a house on the main street.

"Scrubs," I said to myself. It was the cleaner Dr. Warren mentioned. I decided it was worth a conversation.

I pulled over and parked behind the Ford Focus. I cast a wary eye at the grocery bags in my basket. The temperature hovered around fifty degrees; it wasn't July's sweltering heat and humidity, so they should be okay.

Once at the front porch, I tried to take two steps at a time and quickly learned my lesson when I tripped and went sprawling across the wooden slats. Great. To add insult to injury, I probably had a splinter that would get infected and end up costing me another doctor visit.

I climbed to my feet and dusted off my hands, hopeful that no passersby got a view of my backside as I went flying through the air. What was I thinking by trying to put a spring in my step? I was no longer a nubile twenty-five-year-old.

The internal door was open so I rapped on the external door and waited. A portly woman clad in grey sweatpants and a flannel shirt wandered to the door with a dustpan and brush in her hand.

Her expression was quizzical as she opened the door. "Can I help you?"

"Hi, are you Casey Schultz?"

The woman's quizzical expression morphed into a scowl. "Who's asking?"

"I'm Mia Thorne. Hazel Thorne was my father's aunt."

Her features softened. "Right. The great-niece. I'm sorry about Hazel. She was a nice lady. Quirky but nice."

"I understand you worked for her."

"Oh, were you hoping to continue the service? Because I've already filled her spot. I had a waiting list, you see. No point in delaying."

"No, nothing like that." Although now that she mentioned it, hiring a cleaner didn't sound like such a bad idea. I wasn't the neatest person in the world. Of course, I'd prefer to hire someone I was sure wasn't a killer.

"Come in before you catch a cold." Casey ushered me into the foyer. It was a beautiful house filled with gleaming mahogany furniture and oil paintings. A grown-up's house.

I closed the door behind me and cut right to the chase. "Have you heard the sad news about Gladys?" I watched her closely for any sort of reaction, but I saw only sadness reflected in her brown eyes.

"Of course. Who hasn't? A terrible tragedy. And so close to Hazel's death, too." She clucked her tongue. "I'm not sure what could've happened."

"The police arrested her nephew," I said.

"Can't imagine why. Gladys was as sweet as they come and Kurt was just like her."

"Did you clean her house, too?"

"No. Gladys was a spry thing for her age. Liked to keep her own house."

"Did you ever notice anyone lurking around Red Clover that didn't belong there?" I asked.

Casey shifted the dustpan and brush to her other hand. "Not that I can think of. Sometimes the odd package would be delivered. Hazel spent a lot of time in that garden of hers, even in the dead of winter, so if someone was prowling around the grounds, she'd have spotted them before they got too close." She squinted at me. "You think someone killed Gladys because she found them lurking in the yard? I suppose it's possible. Red Clover's been sitting empty for months."

She pointed the dustpan at me, her eyes shining. "I bet I know who's been sneaking around outside. That Scarlet York's been skulking around there for years trying to get her hands on Hazel's garden. She and that friend of hers—the one who dresses like he's taking Celine Dion's place in Vegas—they're probably in cahoots."

"So the two of them weren't actually friends with Aunt Hazel?" Had they explicitly claimed to be her friends, though? I didn't think so.

Casey considered the question. "They were on friendly terms. I don't mean to suggest otherwise, but Hazel didn't invite them 'round for meals or anything."

Her statement gave me pause. I'd only been at Red Clover for all of two seconds when they appeared to welcome me to Newberry. What if Gladys had spotted them trespassing and words were exchanged? What if their interest in me was more sinister than I realized?

I chewed my lip, thinking. Ophelia seemed to like them, especially Patrick. Surely the cat wouldn't act that way if she'd seen them murder Aunt Hazel's dear friend. I felt the tension begin to claw at my stomach. I didn't want to be suspicious of every single person I met in Newberry, particularly the two people who seemed most keen on befriending me.

Unless they were only making an effort in order to cover up their own dastardly deed.

No. It wasn't possible. Scarlet and Patrick weren't capable of such a heinous act. Although they were different from the sort of people I usually hung out with, I trusted them.

Then again, I'd trusted Andrew and look how that turned out. Some gift of intuition I supposedly had.

I shook off the weight of suspicion. I'd spent enough time with Scarlet and Patrick to feel confident they weren't involved. Besides, what motive could they possibly have?

"How often were you at Red Clover?" I asked.

"Once a week most weeks except major holidays," she said with a note of pride.

"Is there anyone you can think of who might have a reason to harm Gladys? Any name you heard mentioned in connection with her?"

Casey blew a wayward strand of hair out of her eye. "You should talk to J.D."

"Who's that?"

"Her gentleman friend," Casey said. "From what I heard at Hazel's, he came around to see Gladys a couple times a week for lunch. Sometimes they went out to dinner."

"Ooh, that kind of gentleman friend."

"Hazel thought things were more serious between them than Gladys let on."

"Why would Gladys downplay it?"

"She was a respectable lady, and I think she worried the relationship might upset people. Her husband had been a well-liked man, you see."

"How long ago did her husband die?" I asked.

Casey waved the dustpan and brush. "Must be going on ten years now. Certainly long enough to be moving on to another relationship. And J.D. was sweet on her." She pursed her lips. "Maybe he got tired of waiting, you know? Men can be like that."

Yes, men certainly could.

"Thanks, Casey. I appreciate your candor."

"No problem. If you want me to add you to the waiting list, just let me know."

"Fair warning. You'll have your work cut out for you."

Casey smiled. "Haven't met a house yet that I can't handle."

According to public records—and by that I mean the internet—'J.D.' stood for Jonathan DuBois Goodman and he worked part-time in a local antique shop called The Golden Key.

He was a tall man with thick white hair and a matching beard. His cheeks were slightly pink, as though he was either excessively cheerful or had recently enjoyed a drink.

"Welcome," he greeted me. "In the market for anything in particular?"

"I just moved into a new house, so I'm getting ideas."

"I'm envious. I love a blank slate."

I faced him directly. "I'm Mia Thorne, the new owner of Red Clover."

A mixture of emotions rippled across his features. Understanding. Confusion. Sadness.

"Gladys," he said softly.

"Did you know her?" I asked.

His eyes moistened with tears. "Yes, very well. In fact, we were supposed to get together the night she died. She recorded episodes of *The Great British Baking Show* and then waited until we could watch them together."

"But you didn't see her?"

"I called to make sure we were still on, but she didn't call me back."

"Why not show up anyway if you had plans?"

His face reddened. "I thought she might be upset with me, so I didn't want to push it."

Aha. "Or maybe *you* were upset with *her*? Went over and killed her in a fit of rage?"

He shot me a quizzical look. "I understand the police have arrested Kurt."

"Not everyone thinks Kurt is guilty."

"But they found the murder weapon with his prints," he objected. His eyes narrowed. "Is that why you're really here? To interrogate me? Are you really a relative of Hazel's?"

"I am, and Gladys was a good friend of hers, and was killed on my property, so I can't help but feel invested."

"What's your theory? I killed Gladys, dressed her in her coat, and drove her over to Red Clover where I left her in the garden?" J.D. shook his head. "Not likely."

"But not impossible if you wanted to delay the discovery of the body. The coat was because you're still a dyed-in-the-wool gentleman, albeit a murderous one. Maybe you wanted more and Gladys wasn't inclined. Bruised your ego. Men have killed for less."

J.D.'s eyes glazed over and sadness seemed to overtake him. "I think you'll find it was the other way around."

My head snapped to attention. "Gladys wanted the relationship to progress?"

He sighed gently. "She wasn't content with the way things were. She wanted to move in with me."

"She told you this?"

He nodded. "We had a long conversation about it a couple weeks before she died. She'd overcome whatever concerns she had about remarrying. She hoped to marry me. We'd move into my house and she'd leave her house to Kurt."

"Did it surprise you that she was leaving everything to Kurt?"

He shook his head. "She loved Carlton dearly, but she never felt like he needed her, not the way Kurt does." He paused. "Or did. Kurt was the baby duckling that constantly needed coddling and Gladys loved to coddle."

"But you didn't want that?"

J.D.'s expression was sorrowful. "I enjoyed our companionship, but I never viewed us as a married couple. I know some older folks marry for lesser reasons than love, but I've never been interested in that. I only want to make it official with someone if I'm head over heels."

"And you told her that?" Ouch. Poor Gladys.

"I think it was Hazel's death that inspired the idea, to be honest. She started picturing a life alone and it didn't appeal to her."

"How did she take your answer?"

"It wasn't an easy thing to tell her. I cared for Gladys very much, but I wasn't about to marry her simply because she was sad and scared."

"How did you end things?" I asked, genuinely curious. Had J.D. done the honorable thing of breaking off the relationship or did he take up with someone new behind Gladys's back like Andrew?

"We agreed to continue the friendship," J.D. said. "I could tell her feelings were hurt, but we enjoyed our time together too much to put an end to it completely."

I eyed him closely. "Have you started dating?"

"No, I'm not keen on dating. If I happen to meet someone I like, then fine, but I'm not going out of my way."

"I suppose Gladys knew your attitude about dating." That was likely the reason she agreed to continue as is. She knew it was unlikely J.D. would meet anyone he liked better.

His eyes danced with amusement. "Oh, yes. We knew

each other very well. In a way, it was a shame I couldn't generate the necessary feelings for her. We made quite a pair."

"Any idea who might have wanted to hurt her? It doesn't sound like she was unpopular."

"On the contrary, Gladys was a breath of fresh air."

I mulled over our conversation. "What do you think of Kurt, other than the fact that he needs coddling?"

"He's a sweet enough fellow. A little too soft, in my opinion."

"When you say she coddled him, what else did she do? Give him money?"

"Sometimes."

"Is it something you fought about?"

He chuckled. "No. Gladys and I rarely argued. Kurt's her family and how she handled her money was her business. I gave her my opinion, of course, and she accepted it graciously. It's one of the reasons we got along so well. Neither of us got our noses out of joint over a difference of opinion."

I smiled. "Sounds like you really had a rock-solid friendship."

Tears brimmed in his eyes. "I can't tell you how much I'm going to miss her."

"Any regrets about shooting down her proposal?"

He blinked away a stray tear. "A little. I would've liked to know that she died happy. She deserved that much."

"I guess you have an alibi for the time of death."

"I'll tell you what I told Chief Tuck—I was home alone, trying to install a new mailbox. Some kids had beaten the old one with a baseball bat as part of some neighborhood hijinks and I was tired of looking at it."

"You must've needed tools for that."

"Of course. I had to put in a new post. That's the hardest part."

"You didn't have help?"

He squared his shoulders. "I know I'm advancing in years, but I'm still capable of the odd job around the house."

"What do you use to install a mailbox?" I asked, just in case I found myself in a similar position.

"You needn't ask. The police already checked my tools for evidence before they found the baseball bat with her DNA. I was relieved, I'll say that much. I had a brief worry that someone might've tried to frame me if they'd known about our recent disagreement."

"Do you think the killer is someone she knew?"

He lowered his gaze. "I wish I knew. It's hard to imagine someone who knew her bludgeoning her like that. They'd have to be cold and heartless and I can't say I know anyone who fits that description."

I shook his hand. "Thanks for talking to me, J.D. It was a pleasure to meet you."

"Let me know if you see anything you like. Everything on the left side of the room is twenty percent off."

I wasn't about to buy an antique without Patrick's approval. No way did I want to bring anything back to Red Clover with a spirit attached to it, although I still wasn't sure I believed any of it. I mean, I believed Patrick's actions were sincere, but I doubted the spirits existed. They were simply all part of his dramatic flair.

I left The Golden Key and headed for home. I'd ruled out Casey and J.D., which meant that Kurt was about to spend another night in prison.

CHAPTER FIFTEEN

I SPENT the evening rooting around the cottage, searching for tarot cards and other items that someone who offered Hazel's 'services' might store. I discovered a bulletin board in one of the spare rooms and decided to use it as a murder board, adding names of suspects, their motives, and opportunities. Maybe having the information in one place would spark an idea.

The phone pinged and I groaned when I saw 'Nurse Ratched' on the screen.

"Hi Mom."

"You haven't called me. I guess that means you're busy settling in."

"You can say that."

"Meet any nice people yet?"

"Patrick and Scarlet have been really helpful." I had no intention of telling her about my date with Dane or the murder investigation or I'd never be able to end the call.

"And what do they do?" she asked.

As usual, my mother was more concerned with knowing

what someone does for a living than knowing what kind of person they are.

"Scarlet owns a landscaping company."

"That's good. And Patrick? Is he single?"

"Patrick is younger than me, hotter than me, and gayer than me."

My mother's disappointment seeped its way through the phone. "He might not be completely useless. Maybe he can offer you a job."

I stifled a laugh. "Not unless you want to tell your friends I've become a ghost whisperer."

"What?"

Crap. I shouldn't have said that.

I cleared my throat. "Patrick communes with the spirit world."

Her distaste was audible. "I guess it makes sense that Hazel would surround herself with people like that. She probably seemed normal there."

"Newberry is an interesting mix of people," I said. "There are lawyers and accountants and…ghost whisperers."

"Then for heaven's sake, seek out the lawyers and accountants. This is a golden opportunity for you to make a fresh start, Mia. If you make the wrong kind of connections right off the bat, you'll never fit in."

"I'm not fourteen, Mom. I don't need to fit in."

A buried memory shot to the surface of fourteen-year-old me warning my neighbor, Helen, not to drive her car after a strong feeling of dread came over me. Helen had driven anyway and ended up in a fender bender a few miles away. She'd told my mother about the incident, who'd dismissed it as a coincidence. I'd felt foolish afterward and worried what people think if they heard about it. My mother's influence, I realized now.

Our conversation put me in a sour mood and I climbed

into bed still grumbling to myself. I was forty-two. Why did I let my mother get under my skin? She was the only family I had—why did our relationship have to be so complicated?

When sleep finally came, it was fitful, littered with nightmares about zombies taking over the town and trees morphing into giants hungry for the taste of human flesh.

I woke up with a start, drenched in sweat. Although the room was still dark, I felt a presence next to me. I waited a moment for my eyes to adjust. I saw a smudge on the neighboring pillow.

"Ophelia?"

The blurriness dissipated, revealing my companion.

I screamed and scrambled out of bed, keeping one eye trained on the figure. My heart thundered in my ears. The horrible doll from Patrick's haunted collection was *in my bed*.

I tried to regulate my breathing. "Susie, what are you doing here?"

The doll stared at me, its yellow eyes unblinking.

"So, um, how did you get here?" I kept my voice even, although my insides were screaming. This doll had somehow transported itself from Patrick's house to mine. Granted, it was only two houses away, but last time I checked, dolls didn't move of their own accord.

Susie remained silent. And motionless.

With a trembling hand, I reached for the phone on my bedside table and texted Patrick.

It's 3am. Do you know where your doll is?
Who is this?
Mia! And your doll is in my bed.
Why are you sleeping with my doll? I thought she freaked you out.

I tapped the screen and called him. My outrage demanded a voice. "I did not put the doll in the bed, nor did I bring that thing into my house."

"Huh. That's odd."

My tongue stuck to the roof of my mouth. "You think?"

"Susie has never left the collection room. I wonder why she would come to your house."

"Patrick, we are talking about a doll. Dolls can't walk."

"Did you forget the part where she's imbued with the spirit of a former owner?"

"I don't care if she's imbued with tequila and amphetamines. *She's a doll* and you told me yourself she couldn't walk."

"Take it as a compliment. Susie has never left the chair for anyone before. She must've taken a shine to you."

I stared at the doll's glassy eyes. "Is this one of those alien host situations? Maybe Susie sees an opportunity to be reborn in my body?"

Patrick laughed. "If Susie was looking for a second wind, I doubt she'd choose someone who gets winded after one flight of stairs."

"Hey! I told you I'd been exercising before that."

"And I told you that riding an electric scooter doesn't count as exercise."

I hung up on Patrick and continued to watch the doll, uncertain what to do next. I was afraid to look away and look back again, only to find that Susie had moved closer to me. The doll was solidly made. I had no doubt she could put up one helluva fight.

The soft patter of footsteps drew my attention to the doorway. Ophelia entered the bedroom and jumped onto the bed with surprising grace. It was like watching a hippo perform *The Nutcracker*.

I waited to see the cat's response to my unexpected guest. Ophelia ignored the doll and meowed at me.

"Yes, I know," I said.

The phone bleeped and I saw Patrick's name on the

screen. "Did the guilt get too much? Have you called to confess?"

"No, but I think I know who to blame."

"I don't think Scarlet is capable of a prank like this."

"Check your cat's paws."

I frowned. "For what?"

"Mud. It rained earlier and there are paw prints in my house."

I gazed skeptically at the cat. "Paw prints that lead into the collection room?"

"Just check."

I didn't have to. One glance at the bedspread told me what I needed to know. "Are you telling me that Ophelia went over to your house with the express purpose of dragging that monstrosity back to my bedroom as a torture device?"

"Well, I can't pretend to know her reasons, but she seems to be the culprit."

I gripped the phone. "She's a cat. She doesn't have reasons!"

Ophelia hissed at me.

"Mystery solved. Good night!" This time Patrick hung up first.

I flung the phone onto the bed and watched it bounce. "Why would you do this?" I asked the cat. I didn't know why I bothered to ask. It wasn't as though she could answer in a language I understood.

"You're like a feline ninja." Ophelia somehow managed to sneak out of the cottage, walk to Patrick's house, drag the doll out of the rocking chair and all the way back to my bed. I remembered a story my father told me about his childhood cat, Sampson. Sampson had killed a bird in the yard and was so proud of his accomplishment that he'd bitten off the head and delivered it to my grandparents' bed as a trophy.

I observed the cat. "Is that what this is, Ophelia? Some sort of trophy? Are you showing off for me?"

The cat rolled onto her back and I worried she wouldn't be able to get back on her feet. Her belly was so big that the fur spread like a fresh pancake on the griddle.

I held a hand cautiously over the bed. "Do you want me to pet you?" I worried the first time had been a fluke.

Ophelia meowed softly, appearing to welcome a show of affection. It felt like a trap. Slowly, I lowered my hand to make contact with her jelly belly. She made no move to bite me. Instead, my hand vibrated.

Ophelia was purring again.

I had no clue what to do about the doll. Ophelia clearly thought she'd done something good by carrying it here. If I got rid of Susie, the cat might view it as an insult and we'd be back to square one.

I sighed. I was exhausted and wanted nothing more than to crawl back under the covers and go to sleep. My gaze darted to the hallway. There were two other bedrooms to choose from. I could leave Ophelia and Susie in here and claim another bed for the rest of the night. It wasn't an ideal solution, but there was no way I was sharing a bed with these two. They had *nightmare* written all over them and I'd had quite enough of those for one night.

The next morning Patrick turned up on my doorstep with an oversized container of coffee.

"Wow. I'm not sure what I was expecting, but this look delivers so much more than my imagination could muster."

I held out my hands in anticipation. "Gimme."

"It was the least I could do," he said, handing over the caffeine. "I imagine Susie kept you awake."

"I decamped to another bedroom for the night." I took a long, luxurious sip of coffee. "What kind of creamer?"

"Peppermint."

I sipped again and felt my body slowly come back to life. "Ophelia seems to think she made me proud. I feel like I'm supposed to hang Susie on the fridge with a magnet or something."

"There's a surefire way to lose weight."

No kidding. I'd bypass the refrigerator until I was on the brink of starvation.

"I consider it a good omen," Patrick said.

"That's because you like the doll."

"I'm not talking about Susie. I'm talking about the fact that Ophelia brought you a gift. It means she's warming to you."

"What will she bring if she really likes me? Herpes and a side of creamed corn?"

Patrick scrunched his nose. "Ew. Creamed corn is the devil's work."

I pressed the container against my cheek and inhaled the rich aroma. "I like how you skipped right over herpes."

"By the way, you've got mail and, judging from the floral aroma, it's not from Tom Hanks." Patrick handed me a manila envelope.

I didn't need to read the perfect script to know who it was from. This envelope had my mother's scent all over it.

"She sends me perfume samples from the store," I said.

Patrick watched me eagerly. "Anything I might like?"

I ripped open the envelope and peered inside. As predicted, there were a handful of different fragrances in tiny sample bottles, along with sample moisturizers and a travel mascara.

"Are you sure you don't like your mother? Because I think she and I would get along famously."

"It isn't that I don't like her," I said. "She's my mom. She's supposed to annoy me."

Patrick shot me a curious look. "You know that's not actually true, don't you? Plenty of people like their moms without getting consistently annoyed by them."

I dumped the contents of the envelope on the counter and let Patrick rifle through them. He happily took the lion's share of the samples, leaving me two small bottles of floral perfume.

"I prefer earthier scents," he said, by way of explanation.

I sniffed the bottle. "I guess I should get used to floral aromas. I'll be surrounded by them soon enough, assuming I can get this garden in shape."

"Yeah, no offense but I don't see that happening anytime soon."

"Thanks for the vote of confidence." I spritzed the air between us.

Patrick wrinkled his nose in disgust. "Much too rosy. It screams kaftans and wine."

"What's wrong with that?"

He gave me a deadpan look. "Nothing if you're an aging debutante."

I shoved the samples into my purse. "I'll keep them handy in case one of your dolls accosts me."

"What should we do about Susie? Am I taking her home?"

"Please. I'll have to move if she stays and then I'll lose my inheritance."

"Why do you think Hazel added that provision?" Patrick asked.

I shrugged. "I guess she wanted me to give this place a chance and the only way to do that was to keep me here for a specified period of time." It was like she knew me, even though she didn't.

I walked into the living room and stopped short. Susie sat on the sofa with a throw pillow nestled behind her.

"O unholy night," I breathed, my palm flat against my chest. My heartbeat thundered between my ears.

Patrick appeared beside me. "She certainly seems to be making herself at home."

"I really wish she wouldn't." I scanned the living room for the cat. "Ophelia, where are you?"

There was no response.

"No worries. I'll take her from here." Patrick swept Susie off the sofa and held her like a small child.

"Do me a favor and strap her into the rocking chair when you get home. I don't want any repeat appearances."

"Tell that cat of yours to keep her sticky paws to herself."

"Deal."

I was relieved to see the back end of Susie the creeptastic doll. If I never saw those glassy yellow eyes again, it would be too soon.

CHAPTER SIXTEEN

AFTER MY DIFFICULT NIGHT, I spent the day on the sofa, watching Bravo and nosing through a few decks of tarot cards I discovered in a kitchen drawer. There was a set with bright rainbow colors, another one with a muted vintage design, and a third one that featured a diverse and stylish cast of characters. Other than admiring the artwork, I had no understanding of the cards and I was too tired to research them online.

Ophelia emerged from the kitchen, her tail swishing back and forth.

"Is that tail thing a form of communication?" I added the question to my mental list of online searches. I had so much to learn.

The doorbell rang and I nearly dropped the phone.

"I really have to get used to that," I grumbled. Nobody in the city ever came to my door unexpectedly. At most, they texted me from the sidewalk outside the building to announce their presence.

I dragged myself to the door, stepping over a throw

pillow that had fallen off the sofa. Ophelia followed me, apparently curious to check out my visitors.

I opened the door to find Patrick and Scarlet on the doorstep.

"Did we have plans to go out?" I asked. Patrick's outfit suggested an evening of drinking and dancing.

"No, we have plans to stay in," he said.

"Your feather boa tells a different story." I flicked his black accessory.

"May we come in?" Scarlet asked.

I backed away to let them pass and nearly tripped over Ophelia in the process. The cat waddled away like a penguin fleeing a crack in the ice.

"What's up?" I asked.

"First, I'd like to offer you this." She held up a bud vase. With their white petals and yellow centers, the flowers looked like daisies.

"Are you trying to overwhelm me?" I asked.

Scarlet glanced at the vase. "What do you mean?"

"You already gave me the aloe plant to keep alive. This just feels like tempting fate."

She relaxed into a smile. "No, these are chamomile for your nightmares."

"How did you know…?" I glared at Patrick. "Is nothing sacred?"

He raised his chin a fraction in subtle defiance. "Sorry, I didn't know it was a secret."

"Keep this on your bedside table and it will keep the nightmares away," Scarlet said.

I accepted the vase and hurried upstairs to put it in its prescribed place. I didn't want to admit it, but I was willing to try anything to avoid another spate of terrible dreams.

When I returned downstairs, Patrick and Scarlet had migrated to the kitchen.

"I'm sorry. What is this?" Scarlet asked. She was studying the bulletin board covered with pictures and information related to the investigation.

"My murder board."

She snorted. "A murder board?"

I pointed to the image of the grey-haired man in a collared shirt that I cut out of one of my aunt's catalogs. "That represents J.D., Aunt Gladys's gentleman friend."

"Why is there a big black X over the picture?" Patrick asked.

"Because I've ruled him out."

"This is both deranged and kind of cool," Scarlet said.

"All the best television detectives have one," I said.

Scarlet studied the board. "Somehow I doubt Chief Tuck has one of these in his shed."

Patrick made a noise at the back of his throat. "Why don't we explain to Mia why we're here?"

"Right." Scarlet shifted uncomfortably. "We'd like to have a talk with you."

"About?" I prompted.

"You, jellybean," Patrick said.

Scarlet glanced toward the living room. "Maybe we should sit down for this."

I felt uneasy. Maybe Casey Schultz had been right and they were about to reveal they'd killed Gladys.

"Is this about the murder?" I asked, my stomach churning.

Scarlet seemed mildly surprised. "No."

I eyed them closely. "Is this a wine conversation or a tequila shots conversation?"

They consulted each other.

"Do you have any fireball?" Patrick asked.

"I think tea will do," Scarlet said.

"Spoilsport," Patrick whispered.

"I'll take care of it." I filled the kettle and set it on the burner.

The fact that Scarlet suggested tea gave me pause. "Is this some kind of intervention? Because I don't need one of those. I swear I black out long before I do anything stupid." Most of the time.

Patrick frowned. "It's not an intervention, but based on what you just said, it might be a good idea."

"We only drank with you at Jama and you weren't sloppy drunk," Scarlet said.

That was true. Thanks to Ophelia, I'd been off booze since the day I found Gladys.

Patrick placed his hands on my shoulders and looked me in the eye. Man, were his lashes amazing.

"We want to make it clear that we're your people," he said.

"My people?"

"Yes. Do you understand?" Patrick stared at me intensely.

"Ohhh. My people." I broke into a broad smile.

Patrick released me. "Yes. We want you to know you have a safe space with us."

"That's really sweet of you, but I'm not gay. I mean, I've had the occasional fantasy about Angelina Jolie in her Tomb Raider outfit, but who hasn't? The woman is a goddess."

Patrick and Scarlet wore matching frowns.

"We're not talking about you raising a rainbow flag." Patrick reached for my hand. "We're talking about magic."

I patted his hand and let go. "I'm sure it is magic—for you. But I like a nice set of pecs and a nice, big…"

Patrick silenced me with a look. "Don't distract me. I'm trying to make a point."

"You're not doing a very good job of it," I said.

Scarlet chewed her lip. "Hold on. I think show-don't-tell is in order."

I looked at her. "I thought it was don't ask, don't tell?"

She shook her head and reached into her bright blue tote bag, producing a book. "Here. This should help."

I opened the book and scanned the top of the page. "Top Signs You're A Witch. Is that some kind of Harry Potter handbook?"

"No," she scoffed. "This is for real witches."

I rolled my eyes. "Oh, yes. *Real* witches."

Patrick read over my shoulder. "Animals are attracted to you."

"I suppose that's true. I haven't lived anywhere that didn't involve a mouse or two. And there was that rat that followed me in the subway one time, but I think it was because of the chili cheese fries I was eating."

"You notice repeated numbers or patterns," Scarlet said.

My eyes popped. "Ooh, yes! I love when the clock on my phone says 11:11. Twice a day!"

"You had an obsession with fairies as a child," she continued.

I clutched my heart. "Hell, yes. I was convinced George Michael was going to marry me one day and my mom thought that was hilarious."

Patrick glared at me. "Steady now."

"You feel drawn to collecting objects such as crystals or shells," Scarlet said.

"I had a shell collection from a trip to Myrtle Beach when I was eight. I managed to keep it for a whole year until my mom accidentally threw it away." I used air quotes around 'accidentally' because I knew perfectly well the act had been deliberate.

"You feel drawn to the moon," Patrick said. "And butterflies always land on you."

I pursed my lips, thinking. "Mosquitoes are basically vampiric butterflies, right?"

"As a child, you liked to make potions," Scarlet said, watching me intently.

"All. The. Time. I used to mix my dad's bourbon with my mom's vermouth and rum." I laughed. "Not the best mixture."

"You feel drawn to nature," Patrick said.

I glanced in the direction of the garden outside the kitchen door. "I did feel kind of connected to those weeds. It's like they need me to thrive."

"You're empathetic," Scarlet said.

I turned to look at her. "That's harsh."

She shook her head. "No, *em*-pathetic. You feel drawn to helping others."

"Ooh, got it." I tapped my chin thoughtfully. "Do I need to score ten out of ten?"

"No, I don't think so," she said.

"That settles it then. I must be a witch." I raised my fist for a bump.

Patrick exhaled. "You're not taking this seriously."

"Are you pouting?" I asked. "It's hard to tell when your lips are already so plump." I heaved a sigh. "Listen, I hate to disappoint you, but I'm not a witch. I'm forty-two years old. I think I would know by now."

Scarlet seemed to contemplate her next step. "Hold on. I came with a backup plan." She plucked another book from her bag. "Here. Open to the bookmarked page and read it to us."

I handed the first book to Patrick and skimmed the contents of the page. "I see a bunch of unfamiliar words, although I recognize one of them from a jar in the pantry."

"Really?" Scarlet moved closer to peer around me. "Where?"

I pointed to the word.

"Huh," she said.

I craned my neck to look at her. "Wait. You can't read this page?"

"No. Can you?"

"Sort of, although it doesn't make sense to me. It looks like a recipe that involves plants and flowers," I said.

"Or perhaps a spell," Scarlet said.

I laughed. "A spell?"

"It makes sense. This is Hazel's book," Scarlet said.

"Then why do you have it?"

"She loaned it to me last year. She thought maybe if I spent some time with it, something might…happen."

My mind was muddled. "Is this a gardening book?"

Patrick groaned. "No, silly."

"It's a special book," Scarlet said, "that can only be read by certain kinds of people." She watched me carefully as though gauging my reaction.

"Literate ones?"

Scarlet ignored me. "I have certain abilities, but they're not organic, not like Hazel's."

"If she was so skilled, then why is her garden such a disaster?"

Scarlet drew a deep breath. "I tried to help, but nothing happened."

I stared at her. "What do you mean you tried to help?"

Patrick lightly smacked her arm. "You didn't tell me that."

She fidgeted with the hem of her top. "I hated seeing the gardens in disarray the past couple months. I knew how much it would upset Hazel to see them in this state, so I came over a few weeks ago and tried to clean them up a bit."

"In that case, I'll have to rethink my offer of having you help me because it's still a mess."

Scarlet shook her head. "You don't understand. The weeds…The flowers…They just ignored me. Everything I did was in vain."

I laughed. "You're saying the garden has a mind of its own?"

"It sounds like she's saying it's a magic garden," Patrick interrupted.

Scarlet lowered her gaze. "I know it all must sound crazy to you. You didn't know your great-aunt. You haven't been raised to believe in…"

Anything, I thought but didn't say aloud. I wasn't raised to believe in anything. Not myself. Not other people. And certainly not in magic.

"But you think the garden will…listen to me?" I asked.

"I think there's a very good chance you'll have the necessary bond," Scarlet said. "The same one that Hazel had. You mentioned that random rose that bloomed."

"But that was a coincidence," I objected.

"Maybe. Maybe not." Scarlet nodded toward the book. "Would it hurt to try?"

"The worst that would happen is you'd feel foolish," Patrick said.

"Well, that's a familiar enough feeling for me," I said. "I'm not opposed to trying." At my age, I thought I knew everything there was to know about myself. It would be exciting to discover untapped potential. And it would be even more exciting to prove my mother wrong. She always made a mockery of anything remotely supernatural. What if my visions and strange sensations over the years actually meant that I had a gift?

"I'll still help you, of course," Scarlet said. "Hazel was knowledgeable about plants. She didn't need me."

"But I do," I said. It wasn't even a question. Besides, I liked Scarlet and Patrick. If I had to stay in Newberry for a year, I wouldn't mind spending it with them.

Scarlet clapped her hands, her dark eyes shining with

excitement. "We'll start with the witch's garden. It's basic and manageable."

"How do we test your theory about me?" I asked.

"We'll monitor any changes in the gardens in the coming weeks. With spring on the horizon, it'll be ideal timing."

"And I will help dress you for the tasks ahead," Patrick said. "You'll need gardening clothes, of course."

I bit back a smile. "Of course."

"Hazel has all the tools you'll need," Scarlet said. "I can teach you how to use them."

A thought occurred to me. "But if I can make roses bloom with the touch of a hand, do I even need tools?"

"I doubt it's that simple. Hazel spent most of her time in the garden," Scarlet said. "She put her blood, sweat, and tears into this place."

I recoiled. "Well, that's disgusting."

Scarlet snorted. "I don't mean literally."

"You can never tell with you two," I said. "Next you'll tell me I need to order an extra supply of eye of newt."

"I have heard it makes an excellent addition to one's anti-aging regimen," Patrick said.

"What about you?" I asked. "Are you some kind of white wizard?"

He adjusted his feather boa. "As much as I like to think of myself as a younger, hotter Gandalf, I'm afraid my skills are limited to the spiritual realm."

"Between us, I think we have all the bases covered," I said.

"The power of three," Scarlet said, smiling.

"Is that a thing?" I asked.

Scarlet nodded. "Yes, it's very much a thing."

"And did Aunt Hazel make a living off her skills?" I asked, thinking of Mimi's visit.

"Let's not get ahead of ourselves," Scarlet said.

Patrick clamped a hand on my shoulder. "All in good time, magical grasshopper."

My stomach rumbled and I realized I hadn't eaten since breakfast. "I need to get some food in me. Anyone else hungry?"

"I think we should go out to eat," Patrick said.

Scarlet gave him a knowing look. "Gee, I can't imagine where you'd like to go."

I glanced from one to the other. "I'm missing something."

"He wants to go to Largo because he thinks the owner is hot."

Patrick lifted his chin haughtily. "And, more importantly, he's very into me."

"I'll drive," Scarlet said.

"Not until you change," Patrick said to me. "You look like you've been used as a tiller in garden."

I brushed aside loose strands of hair. "Fair enough." I went upstairs to make myself presentable. My stomach rumbled again, prompting me to hurry.

Largo was located on the canal side of town and offered a two-tiered terrace that overlooked the water. Despite the colder temperatures, both terraces were jammed with diners.

"We'll be lucky to get a table at all," Scarlet said. "Maybe we should go somewhere else."

"No," Patrick said quickly. "If Jeff knows I'm here, we'll get a table."

We approached the hostess stand and she broke into a smile at the sight of Patrick.

"Hey, stranger. Where've you been?"

"Hibernation," he said. "But I'm slowly reengaging."

"Jeff will be happy to see you," she said. "He's around somewhere."

Patrick leaned forward. "Um, we don't have a reservation, but is there any chance you can find us a table?"

"Yes, of course." She swiveled to face the dining area. "We'll get that table cleaned up for you right away." She smiled at a young man passing by with a dishcloth. "Hector, would you please clean table ten for our guests?" She spoke slowly, enunciating each word.

Hector nodded and maneuvered through the busy room to the table.

The hostess shifted her gaze back to us. "It'll only be a moment."

"Take your time," Patrick said.

We huddled in front of the hostess stand, observing the other guests.

"For a second, I thought I saw Kurt Wiggins," Scarlet said in a hushed tone.

"Nope. Still in jail," Patrick said. "No bail because they think he's a flight risk."

My mood dampened. "Poor Kurt."

A server greeted us with an armful of menus and marched us to table ten where Hector was wiping down the table.

"Oh, please," Patrick said. "You were thrilled when they suspected Kurt."

At the mention of Kurt, the bus boy stopped dead and his hand came to rest on the table.

"I know, but that was before I met him and had a…feeling."

"It's your spidey sense," Scarlet said.

"Or Scooby-sense." I related more to the hungry Great Dane than the lithe superhero.

"All the evidence points to Kurt," Patrick said.

My gaze was on the bus boy who had slowly resumed

wiping the table. He tossed the white cloth over his shoulder and lifted the container stacked with soiled plates.

"Kurt a good man," Hector said in broken English.

I peered at him. "You know Kurt Wiggins?"

He seemed to regret his statement and hurried away with the container, nearly colliding with a server in his haste to escape to the kitchen.

We took our seats, staring after him.

"That was bizarre," Patrick said.

"He knows something," I said.

"Because he knows Kurt or because he knows who really killed Gladys?" Scarlet whispered.

I drummed my fingers on the table. "I'll be honest. Random bus boy was not on my murder bingo card." I started to rise, but Patrick grabbed my shoulder and pushed me back into the chair.

"You can't go back there," Patrick said. "What if he's the murderer?"

"He's not going to kill me in a busy restaurant. Besides, if this guy knows something, I owe it to Kurt to talk to him."

"You don't owe anything to Kurt," Patrick said.

Okay, maybe not, but I still felt compelled to take action. I grabbed my phone.

"I'll text if I need backup. Oh, and order me the fish tacos and an iced tea." I loved the experience of returning to a table and having the food be there.

I walked back to the kitchen. "Hector?" I yelled into the noisy room.

One of the servers exited the kitchen with a tray. "You're looking for Hector Garcia?"

I nodded.

"He just went outside for a quick break." She inclined her head toward a back exit.

"Thanks." I slipped outside into a quiet alleyway where

Hector was smoking a cigarette by the dumpster. I immediately stopped breathing through my nose because I hated the stench of cigarette smoke.

Hector lowered his hand when he noticed me, letting the ash fall from the tip.

"Hi Hector. My name is Mia Thorne. I'd like to talk to you about Kurt."

"Cop?" he asked, eyeing me warily.

I held up my hands, still clutching my phone. "No, I'm not a cop. The woman who died, Kurt's aunt...She was found in my yard, but I don't think Kurt killed her."

Hector drew the cigarette back to his lips in a nervous gesture. Upon closer inspection, he couldn't have been older than twenty.

"Kurt teach me English," he said. "He work at the library."

"Yes, that's right. I met him there." I hesitated, not wanting to say anything that scared him away. "You know something, don't you, Hector? Something that would help Kurt?"

Hector averted his gaze and puffed away on his cigarette. "No."

I'd lived in the city long enough to recognize when a person was dodging the police. Someone like Hector who was young, working in a restaurant, learning English...

I blinked at the bus boy. "You're his alibi," I said quietly.

Hector's brow creased and I realized he didn't understand the word.

"Kurt was helping you with English at the time of his aunt's death, wasn't he?" This explained why Kurt had acted like he was hiding something. He was hiding something all right, but it wasn't murder.

Hector refused to meet my gaze.

"You're afraid that if you go to the police, they'll find out you're an undocumented immigrant." Talk about self-sacrifice. Kurt was more concerned with protecting Hector than himself.

"My sisters. They live with me."

He looked directly at me this time and the fear in his eyes rattled me to my core. Hector was terrified of being deported. If Kurt knew more about Hector's story, it made sense that he would feel compelled to protect his tutee.

"Hector, listen. We'll figure something out. Something that helps Kurt without hurting you."

Wordlessly, Hector tossed his cigarette to the ground and stubbed it out with the heel of his shoe.

And here I thought my exile to Newberry for a year was bad. Kurt's plight certainly put that into perspective. If we didn't figure out a solution, an innocent man was going away to prison for the rest of his life, leaving the murderer to escape justice.

There had to be a way to fix this.

CHAPTER SEVENTEEN

I BARELY SLEPT AGAIN, but at least this time it wasn't due to nightmares. I couldn't wait until morning arrived so that I could pay a visit to the one person I knew could offer advice on the Hector situation.

"Hi Dane." I hovered in the doorway of his office. We hadn't been in contact since our date and I wasn't sure how he would respond to seeing me after my awkward behavior.

Thankfully, he glanced up from his desk and smiled. "Mia. What a nice surprise."

"I hate to spring this on you, but I need to talk to you about a legal matter and it's pretty urgent."

His expression turned solemn and he motioned to the chair. "I have a few minutes. Take a seat."

As I sat, my stomach felt like a miniature zoo for hopping insects.

"Hypothetically, if a murder suspect has an alibi, but they don't want to admit it because it would get the alibi in trouble, is there anything a lawyer can do?"

Dane frowned. "I'm afraid I need a little more information. What kind of trouble?"

I tried to come up with a comparable situation. "Okay, say I found out that Kurt was with a prostitute during the time of the murder, which means he couldn't have done it."

"But the prostitute doesn't want to get arrested so she stays quiet and Kurt doesn't want to get her or himself in trouble either, so they both stay quiet."

"Exactly."

Dane whistled. "Seems like an unfair trade. Nobody's looking at life in prison because of prostitution."

Hmm. Not the best comparison then because the fear in Hector's eyes suggested deportation *could* be a life sentence for Hector and his sisters. If I wanted the best advice, I was going to have to come clean.

"If I tell you something, you have to keep it secret, right?"

Dane studied me. "Unfortunately, I get the feeling it isn't your secret you want to share."

"I know something that can exonerate Kurt. He has an alibi."

"I take it she's not a hooker."

I shook my head. "He's an undocumented immigrant and so are his two sisters who live with him."

Dane blew out a breath. "Got it."

"What are the options?"

He gave me a curious look. "Why do you care?"

I blinked. "Excuse me?"

"I mean you're off the hook. There's a suspect in custody. You don't know Kurt or his alibi. Why put yourself in a difficult situation that has nothing to do with you?"

"I would think you'd understand. Isn't that your job?"

"Exactly my point. It's my job. It's my brother's job. But not yours. And you have no personal stake in the matter."

"I'm not allowed to have an interest in justice and fairness?"

"Of course you are. I didn't mean to suggest…"

"I know Kurt is innocent and now I have the evidence to prove it. What kind of person would I be if I ignored that?"

Dane stared at me for a long moment. "Here's the thing you might not realize about us, Mia. Newberry is a small town. Local law enforcement isn't going to hand over a cooperative witness to the feds for deportation."

"But won't the police be obligated to arrest Hector if they know about him?"

He splayed his hands. "Not at all. Being here unlawfully isn't a criminal offense. It's a civil one."

I sat up straighter. "Then we can help Kurt!"

Dane's smile was like a flash of sunlight that forced me to squint. "I believe we can. Why don't we call my brother together and you can tell him what you know?"

"Okay." I wasn't sure if it was the whole lawyer vibe, but I felt safe in Dane's hands.

I listened as Dane explained the situation to the detective and then put him on speaker so that I could be a part of the conversation.

"Mia came to you first?" Detective Fairfax sounded aggrieved.

"I wanted a confidential opinion," I said, leaning closer to the desk.

"I'll speak to this Hector Garcia," Detective Fairfax said.

"And then you'll release Kurt?" I asked.

"Assuming the information checks out."

I clapped my hands together. "That's terrific news. Thank you so much."

"Wait until it's a done deal," the detective warned. "And then you can thank me by agreeing to dinner."

My brow lifted and I met Dane's surprised gaze. He grabbed a sheet of paper and crumpled it in front of the receiver.

"I think it's a bad connection," he said and quickly hung up the phone.

I glanced down at my lap, frowning.

"I'm sorry," Dane said. "I shouldn't have done that."

"No, it's fine. I'm sure he just did it to annoy you."

"Don't sell yourself short, Mia. He'd be lucky to have you."

I couldn't help but smile.

"So what's wrong?"

"This means the police are back to square one." I thought back to the other suspects I'd spoken to. Maybe it was time to revisit the murder board.

"The key word in that sentence is police," Dane said. He seemed to be reading my mind.

"Thanks for your help. I really appreciate it."

He fixed those Caribbean eyes on me and I nearly melted into the seat. "I'm sorry I haven't called since our date. I got busy with work."

"Yes, your brother mentioned that you can be pretty focused."

Dane's phone rang and he scowled at the sound. "I'm sorry, but I have to get that."

"I totally understand." I rose to my feet.

"Before you go, I wanted to ask—would you be interested in going out again soon?"

My heart skipped a beat. "Seriously?"

"If you don't want to, I understand. You're new in town and probably want to…explore all your options."

The only options I wanted to explore were right in front of me, but I couldn't say that.

"I'd love to go out again," I said. "Text me when you have time."

He picked up the phone with a grin on his face. "For you, I'll make time."

. . .

I arrived home feeling a blend of satisfaction and concern. Kurt would be released and the investigation would continue. I hoped that didn't mean more cops in the yard. I had my own work to do.

I wandered into the study and nearly backtracked when I spotted Ophelia sprawled across a rug, luxuriating in a patch of sunlight. I tiptoed toward the desk where my laptop was already open, keeping one wary eye pinned on the temperamental cat.

"I can take the laptop into the kitchen if you'd rather be alone," I said, sliding into the chair.

Ophelia barely registered my presence, which I took as a sign to stay. I navigated to my bank's website and logged in, squeezing my eyes closed before I could glimpse the current number. Although I hadn't been spending much money since I left New York City, I knew that number would dwindle quickly if I wasn't careful. It was all well and good being the recipient of a house, but it still required funds to pay the bills associated with it.

I peeked one eye open and forced myself to look at the account balance. It wasn't dire. Yet. As long as I stayed home, ate only what I grew in the garden, kept off all the lights, and never socialized with another human being again, I'd manage.

My thoughts turned back to my conversation with Scarlet and Patrick. If I really was some kind of witchy psychic like Aunt Hazel, then maybe I *could* make a living from it. Was the idea so outlandish?

Yes. Yes, it was.

How could I claim to be an expert in an area I knew nothing about? Okay, maybe a smattering of my childhood memories revolved around strange occurrences that my mother quickly dismissed the same way she dismissed the absurdity of wearing turtlenecks in April that were not-so-cleverly designed to hide her facelift.

I had no idea what my magical services would entail, but the thought of working from home in cozy pajamas and watching Bravo while I stirred a few fragrant herbs together definitely appealed to me. No wonder Aunt Hazel lived so long. There was something to be said for not having to worry about meeting basic needs. That bills would be paid. That one bout of misfortune wouldn't bankrupt you. That you would survive. I'd always been one unexpected bill away from disaster. It was a key reason I'd moved in with Andrew so quickly. He owned his apartment so I knew I wouldn't need to worry about paying rent, although I ended up paying for more than I expected. It seemed that Andrew couldn't really afford what he owned. I assumed I'd be able to save money and finally get ahead. I felt like a failure for being financially insecure at forty-two. On the other hand, I lived in one of the most expensive cities in the world and didn't earn a CEO's salary. Without family money to sustain me, it was very hard to get to a comfortable financial place without sacrificing every scrap of pleasure along the way. Without living a life rather than simply existing in one.

I closed the bank website and went into the pantry to explore Aunt Hazel's collection of books. I thumbed through each one on the shelf and found one that mentioned love potions, which made me think of Mimi Van Haren. I paused to read the information more closely. There would definitely be a market for people seeking love.

I pulled out my phone and called Patrick. He answered immediately.

"Is this a butt dial?" he asked.

"No, why?"

"Because that's the only sane reason I can think of for receiving a phone call instead of a text."

I laughed. "You've shown up at my door unannounced. I think that's worse."

"That's friendly."

"And maybe I just want to hear your voice."

He hesitated. "I do have a nice voice, don't I?"

"You really do." It was soft and melodious.

"So what's up?"

"How much do you charge to cleanse a haunted item?" I asked.

"Why? Did you find one? If it's Hazel's spirit, I wouldn't recommend getting rid of it."

"No, I'm thinking about offering my own services and I have no idea what the going rate is."

"Scarlet and I think you might want to hold off on that until you know more."

"Okay, but if I'm going to build a psychic empire from the ground up, I need to know the basics."

"I appreciate your enthusiasm, but I highly recommend putting on the brakes for now."

"So you won't tell me?"

"No, and it's for your own good."

He hung up and I stared at the phone in dismay. Who was he to crush my psychic dreams? I had a long professional history in sales. Lynette used to say I could sell bark to the trees. The trick was convincing a client that they needed what I could provide. As tough as she could be, I appreciated that Lynette had seen potential in me that my own mother didn't. The associated publisher had served as a dysfunctional surrogate mother—another reason that being fired was as hurtful as it was.

I tapped my fingernails on the shelf, my thoughts returning to Mimi. She'd already expressed her needs to me so that part was taken care of. The rest would be simple. If I really had some sort of gift, then I should be able to tackle a simple love spell.

I rummaged around until I found Mimi's number. "Here goes nothing," I breathed.

Mimi arrived at the cottage twenty minutes later, dressed like she was prepared to meet Mr. Right in my kitchen. Her black sequined hoodie sparkled and her wavy red hair was flawlessly styled in a chin-length cut.

"I'm so glad you called," Mimi said. "I've been hopeless ever since Hazel died. She was my relationship barometer." She paused and tapped her chin. "Weathervane? No, wait. Compass. She was my relationship compass."

I reviewed the recipe one last time before I began. I'd retrieved all the ingredients and accessories before her arrival and prayed I didn't screw it up.

"Do you have a particular someone in mind?" I asked.

Mimi drummed her gelled nails on the butcher block. "That sexy beast, Derek Fairfax."

I started to cough. "Derek, the cop?"

Mimi fluttered her lashes. "Isn't he divine?"

"He's also about twenty years younger than you." Honestly, it had to be thirty years, but I didn't want to be rude.

She waved a dismissive hand. "Those older models can't keep up with me. I need a stallion."

I cut a glance at the potential potion. "I don't know that this is an on-demand service, exactly."

Mimi patted my arm. "Just do your best. Shoot for the moon and, even if you don't get there, you'll reach the stars."

"And Derek is the moon in this scenario?" I asked.

She pointed to the blender. "Just get to work."

I dumped the ingredients into the blender.

"Hazel never used modern appliances for this sort of thing."

I hit the button and let the electronic whir fill the air. Mimi gazed hypnotically at the contents of the blender and I felt a pang of guilt. Did she really believe a smoothie would attract a gorgeous younger man like Detective Fairfax? I vowed to learn more about Aunt Hazel's abilities. If I was serious about taking her place, then I needed to truly understand what I was doing.

Scarlet appeared in the kitchen doorway. "Sorry, I knocked." She seemed surprised to see Mimi. "Hey there, Mimi."

"Scarlet, lovely to see you."

I clicked off the blender and poured the contents into a tall glass.

Mimi studied the green liquid. "Should I drink it like a shot or sip it like a fine wine?"

"You're making smoothies, huh?" Scarlet asked and I heard the note of skepticism.

Mimi smiled. "This is no ordinary smoothie, my dear. This is going to attract the next love of my life."

Scarlet narrowed her eyes at me. "Is that so?"

I shifted uncomfortably. "Might be."

Mimi raised her glass in tribute. "Don't be modest, Mia. You've got the gift. You should embrace it."

"I think you mean the grift," Scarlet mumbled.

Mimi sniffed the concoction. "It smells like lawn fertilizer."

Scarlet intercepted the glass before Mimi could bring it to her lips. "I don't think this is such a good idea. Mimi, why don't you leave that glass on the counter?"

Mimi's focus flicked from Scarlet to me. "You don't think I should drink it?"

"No, I think one of the ingredients has gone bad. There's a sour smell." Scarlet maintained a neutral expression.

"You do know your herbs, don't you?" Mimi said.

"Well, we can't have that," I said. I dumped the contents into the sink before Mimi could decide to chance it. She seemed the type.

Mimi collected her purse from the counter. "I guess I'll have to exercise a bit more patience."

"I'm sorry," I said.

Mimi offered a reassuring smile. "It's no problem. I look forward to working with you."

I waited until Mimi left the house to turn back to Scarlet.

"What would've happened if she drank it?" I asked, more than a little scared to hear the answer.

"Probably diarrhea." Scarlet paused. "Or death."

I gasped. "A literal crapshoot."

My mother always said the road to hell was paved with good intentions. This had been a lapse in judgment, although I knew myself well enough to realize it wouldn't be my last.

"Please don't ever do anything like that again," Scarlet said.

"Is this where you tell me that with great power comes great responsibility?"

Scarlet examined me. "Would you disagree if I did?"'

I leaned my elbows on the counter. "I don't know that I'm cut out for this. I've never worked from home or had a job without a 401k and health insurance."

Scarlet patted my shoulder. "Give yourself time to settle in. Things have a way of working out."

"Not for me they don't. You remember how I ended up here, don't you?"

Her lips formed a sympathetic smile. "I think you're here for a reason, Mia, and the sooner you accept that, the happier you'll be."

CHAPTER EIGHTEEN

I WAS THRILLED to receive a text from Kurt the next day. Apparently the police told him that I was instrumental in securing his release and he wanted to thank me personally.

"He's really out of jail thanks to me," I told Ophelia. The cat appeared unimpressed. "I've literally saved a man's life."

The cat lowered her head and closed her eyes. I guess catnip was the only thing that appealed to her.

I rode the scooter to the address he gave me. It was only once I got there that I realized I could've walked. I needed to pay closer attention to Google maps.

I arrived in time to see Stella walking up to the front door. The realtor looked ready to keel over in her stilettos. This was Newberry, Pennsylvania. Why did the older women in this town insist on dressing for dinner on the Orient Express?

"Hey, Stella!"

Stella's brow lifted. "What are you doing here?"

"I was about to ask you the same thing," I said.

"Kurt wants an assessment," Stella replied in her raspy voice.

The realization dawned on me. "This is Gladys's house?"

"That's right." She knocked on the door. "Kurt's already inside."

The door opened and Kurt beamed at us. "Stella, thanks for coming."

"Hi, I'm Mia. You texted me."

Kurt seemed to register my appearance. "You're the woman from the library."

"That's right, but I have a confession to make. I lied about my aunt's name."

Kurt waved me off. "It's okay. The police told me it was the woman who'd inherited Red Clover. I just didn't realize you were one and the same."

"Can we come in or should I have my future deliveries made to your front step?" Stella asked.

Kurt chuckled and stood aside. "Sorry about that."

"You're selling?" I asked, entering the house.

"I'm weighing my options," Kurt said. "You understand how it is."

"I suppose Carlton would've preferred that you use Jax as your realtor," I said.

"He asked, but Aunt Gladys specifically mentions using Stella in her will. I'm not one to go against my aunt's wishes, dead or not."

The house was neat and tidy, exactly what I would expect from a woman named Gladys.

Kurt's gaze swept the room. "Gosh, I really miss her. She's everywhere."

I guess that was the advantage of inheriting a house from someone you didn't know. No memories.

"The kitchen is the best room in the house," Stella said, motioning for us to follow.

"Aunt Gladys was a good cook," Kurt said. "Her meatloaf is one of my favorite meals."

"Now if you decide to sell, you have to remember there will be tax implications," Stella said. "Make a note to ask Carlton for help."

It occurred to me that I hadn't filed my taxes yet for last year and they were due in less than three weeks.

"I know it's kind of late notice, but is there any chance you think Carlton would help me out with my taxes this year? I sort of left it until the last minute and with all the recent changes in my life…"

"After what you did for me, I bet he'd be happy to," Kurt said.

Stella removed another magnet from the fridge. "Here's one of his cards right here." She handed it to me.

I snorted. "On the fridge, no less. It's like the adult equivalent of showing off a good report card."

I tucked the card into my pocket. Wow. A lawyer and an accountant in the span of a week. I hadn't felt this grownup since the time I defrosted the freezer.

Stella frowned and plucked a floral notecard from the refrigerator, clucking her tongue. "That woman is a real piece of work."

"What is it?" I asked.

She held up the note for inspection.

Dear Gladys,

I want to let you know that the easement between our properties needs to be mowed and it's your turn. Please mind my prize-winning azaleas.

Sincerely,
Maureen Englewood

. . .

Talk about passive-aggressive. Despite the pretty stationery, there was an undercurrent of hostility in the message. This easement was plainly an issue between the neighbors.

Kurt read the note over my shoulder.

"Aunt Gladys didn't care for Maureen," Kurt said, "although she thought the husband was pleasant enough."

"Maybe talk to Dane," I said. "See if there's anything you can do about the easement."

"That's an excellent idea," Stella said.

Pain surged through my head and I squeezed my eyes closed.

What on earth was that?

I felt a hand on my back. "Mia, are you okay?"

I regained my composure and looked at Kurt. "Sorry about that. Just a weird brain freeze."

"Oh, I hate that. Sometimes I get one when I have one of those frozen drinks at the movies," Kurt said.

I offered a wan smile. "Yes, it was like that."

A knock on the door took us by surprise. Stella bustled to the foyer to answer it and returned to the kitchen a moment later with a blonde woman who looked to be in her sixties. She wore a tweed coat and brown trousers. Brown leather gloves covered her hands.

"Maureen Englewood," Stella said, "meet your new neighbor, Kurt Wiggins—unless he decides to sell, of course. And this is Amelia Thorne. She's new in town."

"Hazel Thorne was my father's aunt. She died a couple months ago and left her house to me."

Maureen brightened. "Oh, right. Gladys's friend. I was sorry to hear about her."

"And now Gladys, too," Stella said with a mournful shake of her head.

"Yes, a terrible tragedy." Maureen's gaze shifted to Kurt. "I'm sorry for your loss. When I heard they arrested you, I was shocked. I said there's no way you'd be capable of such a despicable act. Everybody knows you don't bite the hand that feeds you."

Thinking of Ophelia, I begged to differ, but I kept my mouth closed.

Maureen bowed her head. "Gladys was my neighbor for twenty years. She'll be missed."

"What brings you here now, Mrs. Englewood?" Kurt asked.

"I saw activity and thought I would see who was here. Make sure it wasn't a squatter or something."

I smirked. Maureen was the quintessential nosy neighbor.

"Just us," Kurt said. "I'm deciding whether to sell or move in."

"While I'm here, it's probably worth mentioning the easement," Maureen said primly. "Especially if there's a chance you might live here."

Kurt played dumb. "The easement?"

"There's a strip of lawn on our side of the fence that actually belongs to both of us. That means we're both obligated to take care of it." Maureen practically harrumphed.

"I don't recall Aunt Gladys ever mentioning that," Kurt said.

"No, she wouldn't, would she? I don't like to speak ill of the dead, but Gladys was taking advantage of Marvin's good nature."

"Marvin's your husband?" I asked.

She clasped her hands in front of her. "Yes. He's at the store right now. He forgot the potatoes for dinner so I sent him back." She shook her head. "Men."

"How was Gladys taking advantage of your husband?" And did I really want to know the answer to that?

"Marvin likes to mow the lawn, so he took care of the

easement," Maureen said, "but he's been spending a lot of time on golfing trips since his retirements."

Gee, I couldn't imagine why.

"It's March," I said. "How high can your grass grow that it became a nuisance?"

Maureen's mouth formed a thin line. "It was high enough to cover my shoes. That's too high."

"And you couldn't mow it yourself?"

Maureen huffed indignantly. "I don't mow."

"But you expected Gladys to mow," I pointed out.

"She didn't have to do it herself," Maureen said. "She could've enlisted the aid of either of her boys, but we shared responsibility and she was shirking hers."

I thought of the floral notecard. "And you let her know, I take it?"

Maureen folded her arms. "We had a conversation about it, yes, after I wrote her a note about it."

"What exactly did you say?" Kurt asked.

"What I told you. That she needed to pick up the slack. She said she'd take care of it," Maureen said. "Then she died. I don't consider that taking care of it, do you?"

Someone was overly concerned with her lawn. It made me wonder what problems she was ignoring in her own life.

"Anyway, I hope you'll be better about taking care of things. It'll be nice to have another man next door."

"Is that the last time you saw Gladys?" I asked. "When you talked about the easement?" I deliberately omitted the word 'argued.'

"As a matter of fact, yes." She didn't sound particularly sad about it. "Life's a funny thing, isn't it?"

I stared at the neighbor for a long beat, waiting to see whether my intuition offered any further information on Maureen Englewood. Nothing happened.

"Is there something wrong with your eyes?" Maureen asked, and I realized she was talking to me.

I relaxed my face. "Sometimes my mascara burns," I lied. "I'm very sensitive."

Maureen inspected my face. "Huh. I wouldn't have known you were wearing any if you hadn't mentioned it. It does nothing for you."

Maureen had clearly attended the Madeline Albrecht School of Compliments.

"I'll be sure to take care of that easement, Mrs. Englewood," Kurt said.

"And I'll make sure it's mentioned in the listing information should he decide to sell," Stella added.

"Thank you," Maureen said curtly. "I'll show myself out."

No one spoke until we heard the click of the front door.

"You don't think…?" Kurt began.

Stella's brow creased. "She's awful, but I don't think she'd follow Gladys to Red Clover and hit her with a baseball bat."

"Then again, she lives next door and the bat was here in the yard," Kurt said. "She could've easily taken it."

"But there were no prints except yours," I said.

"She was wearing gloves," Kurt said.

"She's always wearing gloves," Stella said. "I swear she wears them all the way until Memorial Day. She's cold inside and out."

It was something to consider.

"I should go," I said.

"Oh, let me get your gift," Kurt said. "It's in my trunk."

I gave Stella a polite peck on the cheek. "It was nice to see you again."

"Make sure you tackle that garden now that the police have gone," she said.

"I will." I followed Kurt out of the house and he opened the trunk of an older blue sedan.

"A token of my appreciation," he said, lifting an object from the floor of the trunk. "I have a little money now, thanks to Aunt Gladys. I wasn't sure what would be appropriate, so I just bought a bunch."

It was a gift card tree. Each branch had a gift card clipped to it for what I assumed was a local store.

"Kurt, this is incredibly thoughtful. Thank you."

"I figured you could use them to get to know places in town. Help you acclimate."

"You have no idea how helpful this is." I felt overwhelmed with gratitude. This simple gesture would buy me more time. Help me figure out next steps.

"It's the least I can do," he said. "You saved me from a life sentence."

"I just wish we knew who the real killer was," I said.

He closed the trunk. "Same. It's hard to sleep at night, not knowing the truth."

"It will come out. It always does. Hey, the truth already set you free."

He smiled. "Which means I'll see you around. Maybe at the library."

"I'm warning you now—I'll be a regular there."

I carried the gift card tree to the scooter and placed it in the basket. I was glad Kurt retreated inside the house and missed seeing me nearly smack myself in the nose with the helmet. Graceful I was not.

Unfortunately, I only made it a quarter of a mile before I realized there was a nail in the front tire. I debated pressing onward since Red Clover wasn't far, but I worried about a blowout. In the interest of caution, I coasted to a stop on the side of the road. Now what? I could walk back to the house, but I'd have to carry the gift card tree and I hated leaving the scooter behind. It could be easily stolen and then I'd have no wheels at all.

I texted Patrick and then Scarlet but no response. I considered texting Dane but didn't want to seem needy, even though I was actually in need.

Well, I'd texted my only two friends in town. There was nothing to do now except wait.

CHAPTER NINETEEN

HELP ARRIVED a few minutes later in the form of Chief Tuck and a pickup truck.

"Looks like you need a hand," he said, walking over to investigate.

"Nail in the tire," I said, pointing. "Can you drive me to the auto body? Buddy's Body or something?"

He chuckled. "Nonsense. We can do better than that."

"We can?"

"Sure. We can mend it ourselves." He stood in front of the scooter. "Might want to empty your basket first."

I removed the gift card tree and put it on the floor of the passenger seat. Chief Tuck opened the back of the truck and together we lifted the scooter into it.

"Where are we going?" I asked, once he pulled onto the road.

"My place. I've got everything we need to teach you a valuable lesson."

I laughed. "Sounds ominous."

"Everybody should know how to patch a tire. It's a basic skill."

"I think you'll find I'm lacking many of those."

"You're too hard on yourself. My wife was like that, too. I wonder what we teach girls that they grow up being so tough on themselves."

He turned down a long driveway and a small white farmhouse came into view.

"Your house is like a postcard," I said.

"I don't keep it as nice as my wife used to." He parked in front of a huge shed. "Everything we need's right in here."

The shed was overflowing with…stuff. I counted at least three transistor radios on a table, a set of walkie-talkies on a shelf, two CBs, and a myriad of other gadgets.

Chief Tuck walked over to a table and cinched a tool belt around his red flannel shirt. The tool belt had 'Tuck' etched in the leather strap.

"What's Tuck a nickname for?" I asked.

He peered at me. "Never you mind, young lady."

I glanced around the shed. "This looks like the place where objects come to die."

"No, this is where they come for a new lease on life."

"How many of these have you actually fixed?" I asked.

"There's no rush. I enjoy the process of tinkering."

His phone rang and he reached into his back pocket to answer it.

"You're the chief of police and you use a flip phone?" I blurted. The chief was as much of a relic as everything in his shed.

He shushed me and listened to the caller. "Have Tony take care of it. Thanks." He hung up and fixed his Paul Newman eyes on me. "The more electronic a thing is, the faster it breaks and the more expensive it is to fix. Flip phone serves my purposes just fine."

We removed the scooter from the back of the truck and placed it on the ground. The shade made it harder to see.

Chief Tuck must've noticed me squinting because he said, "You should always have a spare flashlight. Didn't your father teach you that?"

"My father died when I was young. Besides, I don't need one." I activated the flashlight on my phone. "You, too, could have this miracle if you gave up your flip phone."

Chief Tuck gave his pocket an affectionate pat. "I'm all set, thanks." He looked at me with renewed interest. "Your dad died?"

"Yes, a long time ago. That's how I'm related to Hazel. On my father's side. It's one of the reasons I never knew her. I told you it was complicated."

"Your mother didn't encourage the relationship?"

"The only relationships my mother encourages are the ones that result in an engagement ring—for her or me. Doesn't matter which."

He cast me a sidelong glance. "You ever been married?"

"No, but Mom's on her third husband. Maybe this time she'll get it right."

"Do you really believe that?"

"Nope."

He chuckled. "I was married for forty years. Irene wanted me to retire years ago, but I was resistant. Then she died and I saw no reason to stop working."

"I'm sorry. I didn't know."

"Breast cancer. She put off her mammogram by a couple years and, by the time she had it, the cancer was too advanced."

No wonder Chief Tuck was reluctant to give up his work. It was all he had in his twilight years. Well, work, tinkering, and fishing.

"What happens once you fix one of these things? Do you sell it?"

"No, no. I usually donate it or I keep it, depending on

what it is. I like listening to the chatter. Keeps me from getting lonely."

"I can't imagine you're ever lonely in a town like this, not when everyone knows you."

He smiled at me. "You'd be surprised. I do like my solitude, though."

"Is that why you go fishing?"

"That's one reason. I go alone and try to stick to the part of the river where nobody can reach me." He gave me a pointed look, remembering our conversation from my backyard. "Sometimes that doesn't quite work out."

"Next time I see you drifting by, I promise to ignore you."

He grunted. "Good. I appreciate that."

I motioned to the shed. "So is this place your sanctuary?"

Chief Tuck looked around, as though viewing the space with fresh eyes. "I suppose it is."

"Does that mean you'd rather not be bothered in here either?"

"I mind being bothered anywhere, but I'm the chief of police. I don't have the luxury of minding." He gestured to the tire. "We should get back to business. Do you know anything about tires?"

I held up my hands. "Let's assume I don't know how to do anything." I had my super change the lightbulbs in every apartment I'd ever lived in. Chances were good that I didn't know how to do anything he wanted to teach me.

He assessed me. "Yeah, I think that's a fair assumption."

"Don't judge."

Chief Tuck kneeled beside the scooter. "Fair enough. Come down here and I'll show you what to do."

I crouched down and hoped I didn't lose my balance. "Thanks. This is my only mode of transport, so I really need it."

"You've got two legs, don't you?"

"I do and, if I must say, they're my best feature. But there are no sidewalks on the main roads and it would make me nervous to walk in the dark."

Chief Tuck leaned over and examined the injured tire. "Yep, that's a nail all right."

"Is this the same situation as when you're impaled? You're not supposed to pull it out or you risk blood loss?" I glanced at the tire. "Or, in this case, loss of air."

"I guess there's an analogy there. In this case, though, we have to take out the nail or you'll end up destroying the tire."

"We don't want that."

He flicked a glance at me. "It's a commendable thing—what you did for Mr. Wiggins and Mr. Garcia."

"Thanks, that reminds me. I have a new suspect for you. Maureen. Gladys's neighbor."

"Sorry, that's a dead end. We already interviewed Maureen Englewood."

My hopes crumbled. "And I guess you cleared her."

"She has a rock-solid alibi."

"She also has a rock-solid horrible personality."

"Maybe so but, last I checked, being horrible isn't a crime."

"It should at least qualify as a misdemeanor."

He chuckled. "Try not to worry. We're back on the case now that Kurt's been cleared. Detective Fairfax is working in the field and I'm doing mental legwork." He tapped his temple. "I find keeping my hands occupied also keeps my mind occupied. Helps me think through a puzzle."

"You treat a murder investigation like a puzzle?"

"Sure, why not? I do some of my best thinking when I'm fixing or making something. It stimulates a different part of my brain."

"So does weed. Have you tried that?"

He suppressed a smile. "Can't say that I have."

I winced. "It's not legal here, is it?"

His mouth split into a grin. "Don't think it's legal where you come from either."

"No, but it's the city. There are way worse crimes to worry about."

"I'll put your mind at ease, Mia. Newberry may be a small town, but we don't make a habit of arresting people for smoking dope, much the same way that we don't turn over information to federal immigration enforcement agents unless it's in connection with a serious crime."

"Good to know."

"Now the goal here is to remove the nail and plug it. It's not a long-term fix, but it will buy you time before you need to spring for a new tire."

"That's perfect." Another financial savings.

Chief Tuck set out the tools and explained what to do. "Let me grab my gun. It's on the table."

I balked. "You leave your gun lying around?"

"My heat gun," he clarified. "We need it to cure the site."

He returned with the gun and showed me how to use it. I was nervous about burning a hole straight through the rubber, but somehow I managed to follow his instructions.

"All finished," he said. "You're good to go now."

I felt a rush of pride as I surveyed the mended tire. "Really?" My mother wouldn't believe me if I told her, which I wouldn't. She'd only find a way to make me feel stupid.

"Don't forget this." He retrieved the gift card tree from the truck and placed it in the basket.

"This is from Kurt," I said. "A thank you present."

Chief Tuck kept one hand on the basket. "Goodwin," he said.

"Excuse me?"

"You asked about my name. My first name's Goodwin. It

was my mother's maiden name and she wanted me to have it."

"That's nice," I said.

"Always felt too fussy for me. I started going by Tuck when I was a boy and it stuck. My grandkids even call me GranTuck."

"That's sweet. Are they local?"

"Not quite but close enough." He released his grip on the basket. "I wish Irene was still here to watch the little ones grow up. She would've loved seeing them learn how to walk and read and all the other milestones. She was the one who kept the pencil chart on the wall of everyone's heights. I haven't been able to keep it going. Reminds me too much of her."

I started the scooter. "You'll just have to enjoy the kids for the both of you."

He gave me a dour smile. "I guess I will."

Feeling upbeat after my triumph over the tire, I decided to stop by Carlton's office to see if he could squeeze me in for an appointment sometime soon. I wanted to keep the productive momentum going. The office was located on Ferry Road, one of the smaller side streets downtown, and I figured it would be a chance for me to match some of the gift cards to their respective locations.

I parked in the driveway that ran alongside the building. A black Audi was the only sign of life. I removed the gift cards from the tree and stuffed them into my purse. No need to attract any opportunistic thieves.

I entered through the front door and was surprised to see an empty room. No furniture. No artwork. Nothing.

A woman emerged from a back room, gripping a broom.

"I'm sorry. I must be in the wrong place. I'm looking for Carlton Spencer."

The woman directed her gaze to the back room and started to sweep.

"Thank you," I said.

I found Carlton alone, packing files into cardboard boxes. This room was also devoid of furniture.

I knocked on the doorjamb. "I guess this isn't the best time to offer myself as a potential client."

Carlton seemed startled to see me. "Oh, hey. I'm between offices. Maybe give me a call in a week or two."

"Yes, I can see you're in casual mode." I gestured to his mesh shorts and Penn State sweatshirt.

"I came straight from the gym," he said. "Figured I'd shower when I get home since I knew this place would be dusty."

"Did Jax find you a better deal on a lease?" I asked.

"Please don't say anything to Jax," he said quickly.

Okay, that was odd. "You're slinking off like a thief in the night?" I asked, half joking.

"No, I just want to be the one to break the news."

"You're a brave accountant," I said. "Taking a vacation to Mexico *and* moving offices during the busiest time of year." It would be like a teacher taking a vacation in September.

"No risk, no reward, right?" He crossed the room to retrieve another stack of files and I noticed a mark on his calf.

"Ha! We're twins." I removed the bandage from my hand and showed him the wound inflicted by Ophelia.

Carlton glanced casually at the back of his leg. "I'd kept it bandaged to start with, but the doctor suggested I let it air out. Helps the healing process."

"Another souvenir from Mexico?" I asked.

"Jellyfish sting," he said.

Huh. Strange that a jellyfish sting resembled a cat bite. I glanced at my hand again and an idea began to take shape.

A very, very bad idea.

"Is that why you were taking antibiotics the night I met you at Jama?"

"Yeah," he said, nodding. "I saw the doctor as soon as I got back and he put me on them. Said it was standard practice."

Except at Jama, they said he was taking the antibiotics for Montezuma's revenge, not a jellyfish sting.

"Carlton, are you really moving offices?"

He flinched. "Of course. Why would I lie about a thing like that?"

"Because you're embarrassed. Listen, I get it. I lost my job in spectacular fashion. There's even evidence of it on the internet."

"Fine," he said, relenting. "I went to Mexico to drown my sorrows after my business folded. I figured it might be my last chance to live it up for a bit."

"You're an accountant. How could your business possibly go under?"

Carlton licked his lips. "I lost my CPA license."

I sucked in a breath. "Does your family know?"

"Nobody knows."

I remembered him at the bar at Jama in his suit. "You weren't coming from work that night I met you," I said. "You'd been on a job interview."

His guilty look was the only answer I needed.

"It didn't go well, did it?"

Carlton scowled. "Kind of hard to get hired somewhere without a license."

"You must be getting desperate for money. Believe me, I know the feeling. Tell me, Carlton, did you even bother to ask your mom for money before you killed her?"

Carlton clenched his hands into fists. "I hinted around, but she didn't take the bait."

"So you decided it was better to kill her for the money rather than bruise your ego and admit to your mom that you're not the superstar she thought you were?"

His face reddened. "She was an old woman. She'd lived her life. I thought I was her sole beneficiary. I figured I'd use the money to invest in a new business venture. Tell everyone I chose to leave accounting."

"You said you knew that she was leaving everything to Kurt."

"I lied. Of course I didn't know. I'm her son!" Carlton's mouth twisted into an angry grimace. "I knew she felt sorry for him, but I never expected her to cut me out of her will for his sake."

"You played it real cool, I'll give you that much. I believed you." I shook my head ruefully. "You seemed so nice. Why do I always get fooled by the narcissistic butt wipes?"

It was a rhetorical question. I already knew why thanks to the hundreds of articles I'd read online—because my mother was a narcissistic butt wipe and we're drawn to what feels familiar.

"Sounds like a good topic for your therapist." He paused. "Which I'm sure you have in ample supply."

I folded my arms defiantly. "As a matter of fact, I do *not* have a therapist." But only because I excelled at self-diagnosis.

He sneered. "I thought all you city types liked to pay someone to listen to you whine about your fractured childhoods."

"What's your excuse? From what I hear, your childhood was idyllic."

Carlton blew a raspberry. "Do you have any idea the kind of pressure I was under to keep up the pretense? I always had to do everything *right*. Meanwhile, Kurt got to act like a pathetic moron and everybody still loved him."

"I'm sure your mother would've loved you, too, even if she'd known the truth."

His fingers curled tightly around the edge of a box. "I'd finally worked up the nerve to go to her house and ask for money, but she wasn't there, so I called to see where she was. She told me she was walking to Red Clover to feed that stupid cat."

I folded my arms. "Ophelia is many things, mostly in pound form, but she is not stupid."

He pressed on with his story. "She was upset. Crying over that friend of hers she wanted to marry."

"J.D.?"

"Yeah, Mr. British Bake Off. I realized that if she got her way and married him, her money and the house would go to him when she died."

Not necessarily, but I didn't bother to correct him. "And it was then you decided to take action."

"I started to panic and then I saw the baseball bat in the yard."

My breathing hitched at his admission. "Kurt's baseball bat." Carlton Spencer was the definition of a cold-blooded killer. "How fortuitous for you."

"More like typical. Kurt never cleaned up his messes. Good thing it was cold outside or I wouldn't have been wearing my gloves. Pretty ingenious, huh? The bat only had Kurt's fingerprints and my mom's DNA."

"Except you didn't know about his alibi."

His jaw hardened. "No, that was unfortunate. He's such a loser. I assumed he would've been alone. I blame you for this, you know."

"Because I found his alibi?"

"No, because I think it was your great-aunt's death that

sparked the idea," Carlton said. "My mom mentioned that Hazel had left everything to you. How cool it was that her death could change a life for the better."

My hands cemented to my hips. "Maybe my life was just fine and the inheritance only complicated matters."

"Not from where I'm standing," he sneered.

"Right back at you. You let your friends continue to think you're leading a charmed life when you've been headed steadily downhill for years. If only you hadn't been so arrogant, you might've admitted it and gotten help before it became insurmountable, but you had to keep playing the part of the golden boy. I bet your mother intended to leave her estate to Kurt all along simply because she liked him better."

I hit a nerve. Carlton grabbed the box from the desk and heaved it at me. I managed to jump out of the way in time and the box landed on the floor with a thud.

I screamed and hoped the woman was still in the next room. There was no sound of running feet or a door slamming. I was alone with a killer.

My mind reeled. The upside of being prone to anxiety was that I had a plan for such an attack, but I'd assumed it would take place in the basement of an apartment building when I was wearing my earbuds and waiting for my laundry to finish.

Carlton approached me with a menacing glint in his eye. "You should've stayed in the city."

Frantically, I dug through my purse, my heart beating rapidly, until my fingers found the best weapon in my arsenal.

He smirked as he edged closer. "I doubt you've got a gun in there. What's your plan? A tube of sexy red lipstick? Don't bother. It only ages you."

I gasped in protest. The moment he was close enough, I

ripped a sample perfume bottle from my purse and sprayed the floral scent straight into his eyes.

He threw up his hands to shield his face. "What the hell?" he raged.

I bolted from the back room. Carlton came after me, half blind. The woman was gone but she'd left the broom leaning against the wall. It struck me as the ideal weapon for a so-called witch like me. I ran like the ice cream van was about to pull away and gripped the broom by the bristled end. I swung it around in a half circle just as Carlton reached me and whacked him hard in the side of the head. He staggered diagonally and collapsed against the wall, sliding to the floor in a heap. Blood seeped from the wound and an image of Gladys sprang to mind. Like mother, like son.

There was no time to freak out about what I'd done. I hunted through my purse to find my phone. Thankfully, the police station wasn't far. I felt confident that one of them would arrive before the killer regained consciousness.

CHAPTER TWENTY

"Looking good, Wilson," I told the aloe plant. I wasn't sure how I'd managed it, but the little green guy was still standing. One week down; a lifetime to go.

The doorbell rang and I set the watering can on the kitchen counter. Ophelia meowed and followed me to the front door.

"Chief Tuck," I said. "What a nice surprise."

He held out a pink flower. "Spring's around the corner, it seems."

I accepted the offering, bringing it straight to my nose for a sniff. "Pretty. What is it?"

"No idea. Saw it in your garden and thought it would look nice in a vase. Brighten up the place."

"Are you saying this house is gloomy?"

"Well, it's seen its share of darkness recently."

I didn't disagree. "Thank you."

The chief hiked up his trousers. "Just wanted to come by and see how you're settling in." He angled his head in the direction of the garden. "Looks like you've got your work cut out for you."

"It's definitely going to take time, but I have plenty of it."

"I also wanted to say thank you for your help with the Gladys Spencer case."

"No problem," I started to say, but he cut me off.

"But let's not do this again, Ms. Thorne. You're a civilian and we can't have civilians running around playing Sherlock Holmes. You could've been killed."

I flashed a smile. "I don't plan to find another dead body in my garden, so I think we're good."

"If you ever want to go fishing, give me a holler," he said. "I know all the best places on the river."

I jabbed a finger at him. "If I ever decide to be bored to tears, you will be the first person I call."

"There's something else you should know about that cat of yours." He glanced down to where the giant ink blot was spread across the foyer floor.

"What is it?"

"She didn't attack Gladys, only Carlton. According to the autopsy results, there were no bites or scratches on Gladys."

"Then how did she end up with the bacteria in her system?"

"Looks like the cat licked Gladys's wound, probably in an attempt to heal her or maybe comfort her."

"And the bacteria was in the saliva." I let the information sink in. "Ophelia didn't attack them both?"

He hooked his thumbs through his empty belt loops. "Nope. Just the one she considered to be trespassing. She likely came to the woman's aid. Bit him in the calf trying to defend Gladys."

I turned to gaze at the fluffy penguin. "You tried to save her," I said softly. Either that or she desperately wanted her bowls refilled. "Thank you for letting me know, Chief. I appreciate it."

He continued to hover and I could tell he had more to say.

"I can tell you have words of wisdom to dispense. Lay it on me, Chief. I can handle it."

"Be mindful of Fairfax," he said finally. "Derek, I mean."

"Is there a problem with him?"

"No, he's a decent guy. A good cop. But he has the unfortunate habit of going after what his brother wants." He gave me a meaningful look.

"I see."

"Derek's competitive, which is part of what makes him a good cop, but also what makes him a crappy brother. Before you make any decisions, you might want to be sure who's interested in you for the right reasons."

I couldn't help but smile. "Chief Tuck, I'm an unemployed forty-two-year-old with a permanent pouch and an empty bank account. What exactly are the right reasons for being interested in me?"

He tipped an imaginary hat. "You have a nice day, Ms. Thorne."

I closed the door behind him, my mind churning. I'd already gotten the impression that Derek's interest in me was inauthentic, although I couldn't deny I felt a genuine spark between us. I felt bad for Dane, though. If his brother had a habit of going after what Dane wanted...The whole dynamic seemed like a recipe for disaster.

I'd no sooner placed the pink flower in a champagne flute filled with water when my phone buzzed and Dane's name flashed on the screen.

"Your ears must've been burning," I said.

"Oh? Talking about me to that cat of yours?"

"Chief Tuck was here." I bit my lip. "He was saying what good guys you and Derek are." I decided to keep the rest to myself.

"That's high praise."

The doorbell rang and I turned back toward the door.

"Give me one second," I told Dane.

I opened the door. Dane stood on the front step with the phone to his ear. "I was wondering if you'd like to have dinner tomorrow night. My treat."

My heart thumped in my chest. "You're here."

"I couldn't decide whether it made more sense to call or invite you in person, so I did both."

A small laugh escaped me. It was the kind of thing I would do when faced with indecision.

"I'm glad you're okay. Derek told me about what happened with Carlton."

"Thanks, I'm glad, too."

His mouth quirked. "Did you really beat him with a broom?"

"I really did."

"I didn't peg you as woman with a violent streak." He heaved a dramatic sigh. "You can take the girl out of the city…"

"I don't make a habit of attacking people."

"Let's hope not, although I heard he smelled wonderful when he got to the station. Everybody wanted to know the scent he was wearing."

I laughed. "You can thank Madeline Albrecht for that. She always said I needed more perfume in my life. I guess she was right for once." Not that I'd ever admit it to her.

"So we're on for dinner?"

I couldn't believe my luck. Forget the nonsense with the garden and the books. *This* had to be magic. There was no earthly way this incredibly hot, incredibly intelligent man wanted to go out with me. Again.

"Yes," I said.

He lingered on the step. "Before I go, there was something I meant to do the other night, but the moment got away from me." His sea-colored eyes gazed at me with a quiet intensity. "Would it be okay if I kissed you good night now?"

I broke into a huge smile. "It's the middle of the day."

He shrugged. "I'm behind schedule."

I pretended to mull it over. "This could be the cure for the nightmares I've had."

"Ah, so that's your reason for agreeing."

I offered a shy smile. "I can think of at least one more."

I stood on my tiptoes to close the distance between us. Dane's head dipped down and his lips met mine. They were soft and gentle and exactly the way I imagined they'd feel.

As we broke apart, an image flashed in my mind of this precise moment and I realized this was the kiss from my vision. I hadn't glimpsed the end of our first date. I'd glimpsed *this*.

"I'll pick you up tomorrow at seven," Dane said.

"I'll be ready."

I was still beaming when I closed the door and turned toward the living room. A flash of white drew my attention to the floor.

"What do you have there, Ophelia?" I asked. I bent down and plucked the sheet of paper from under her paw. How did she manage to drag a piece of paper into the foyer? What was I saying? If she dragged Susie two houses down, she could manage a flimsy letter.

My heart skipped a beat when I recognized the handwriting. It was the missing page of the letter from Aunt Hazel, the one Dane had given me when I arrived.

I carried it to the sofa like it was a bomb I needed to disarm. The first page had left off on a cliffhanger and I was eager to hear the rest of what she had to say. What was the most important thing she wanted me to know? My eyes scanned the remainder of the letter. There wasn't much, but it was more than enough.

You are special, Amelia Thorne, and you come from a long line of special women. Be true to yourself, learn to honor that authentic part of you, and you will always—always—be okay.

Much love,
   Hazel

Emotions wedged in my throat. Aunt Hazel would've been an invaluable asset in my youth. Someone to offset my mother's dismissals and criticisms. I was so sorry to have missed out on a relationship with her.

You are special.

I clutched the missing page to my chest and smiled. "So were you, Aunt Hazel. So were you."

* * *

Don't miss **Life's A Birch**, Book 2 in *The Bloomin' Psychic* series! To keep updated on new releases, be sure to join my newsletter via my website at www.annabelchase.com.

Printed in Great Britain
by Amazon

56189835R00130